Giving Chase

INCENDIARY INK
BOOK ONE

AMY BOOKER

By

Amy Booker

Published by Renaissan Publishing Limited, Cuyahoga Falls, Ohio

www.amybookerauthor.com

Author's Note

If you've read my previous books, you'll know the chapter names are all song titles. Music has been an integral part of my life and always sets the mood for my writing. Whether it's the overall energy of a song, the lyrics, or even the title, that tone carries through into my written words on the page. The playlist and a link can be found at the back of each book, or you can find them on my website: www.amybooker-author.com.

Content Warning

This novel contains adult themes including substance abuse, addiction recovery, complex relationships, and intimate scenes. Recommended for mature readers.

*To the ones whose love story
isn't following the usual script,
whose heart keeps choosing
the harder path—
Some roads are worth the detours.*

"Every heart sings a song incomplete until another heart whispers back."
Plato

Imposter Syndrome

ELIZA

THE STEADY THRUM of my fingernails on the polished mahogany desk fills my office. It's a habit I've never entirely kicked, much like my afternoon espresso or penchant for emotionally unavailable men. I glance at the clock: 2:45 PM. Fifteen minutes until the board meeting, and my mind is anywhere but on the Q4 projections I should be reviewing.

I stand, moving to the floor-to-ceiling windows of my corner office. The Los Angeles skyline stretches out before me, a concrete jungle I've called home for the better part of three decades. At fifty-five, I still cut an impressive figure—tall, with a fuller silhouette that speaks of a life well-lived. My long platinum blonde hair cascades down my back, the ends a vibrant purple that catches the late afternoon sun.

The intercom buzzes, Jenna's voice filling the

room. "Ms. Kerr, there's a call for you on line one. It's about the Rock and Roll Hall of Fame induction."

My heart skips a beat. Damn. I'd hoped the email I'd received earlier was some sort of elaborate prank. "Thanks, Jenna. I'll take it."

I pick up the phone, my voice steady despite the sudden dryness in my throat. "Eliza Kerr speaking."

"Ms. Kerr, this is Daniel Greenblatt from the Rock and Roll Hall of Fame Foundation. I'm calling to formally request your participation in this year's induction ceremony."

I listen as he outlines the details, my mind racing. Incendiary Ink. Hall of Fame. Induction speech. The words swirl in my head, each one carrying the weight of two decades of history, of triumphs and regrets, of stolen kisses and broken promises.

"Ms. Kerr? Are you still there?"

I realize I've been silent for too long. "Yes, Mr. Greenblatt. I'm here. It's just... unexpected news."

"I understand. The band was quite insistent that you be the one to induct them. Particularly Mr. Avery."

Mr. Avery - Chase. The name alone sends a jolt through my system, awakening feelings I'd thought long buried. I see him in my mind's eye: tousled dark hair, green eyes that crinkle at the corners when he smiles, that damn dimple in his left cheek that always made my knees weak. Twenty years ago, he was the twenty-five-year-old rocker who turned my world upside down. Now, at forty-five, he's... what? A man I once knew? A mistake I can't seem to stop making?

"Ms. Kerr?"

I snap back to the present. "Thank you for the call, Mr. Greenblatt. I'll need some time to consider this request. As I'm sure you know, it's not typically done this way."

"Of course. Please let us know your decision by the end of the week."

I hang up, my mind reeling. My imposter syndrome starts to creep in, telling me I don't deserve any of this. Despite the countless sacrifices I've made, especially personally, it feels like I've faked my entire rise into this position. Deep down, I know I've earned it, but that little nagging voice in the back of my head never truly goes away. And the mention of Chase just makes everything worse.

The intercom buzzes again. "Ms. Kerr, the board is ready for you in the conference room."

"Thanks, Jenna. I'll be right there." My voice is low, with a hint of gravel that comes from years of long nights and heated negotiations. And maybe a few too many cigarettes shared with a particular lead singer under starlit skies.

I smooth down my tailored black blazer and straighten my shoulders. Eliza Kerr never shrinks, not for anyone or anything. With one last glance in the mirror—perfect makeup, not a hair out of place—I stride out of my office, the heels of my boots clicking a staccato rhythm as I walk.

The conference room falls silent as I enter. Ten pairs of eyes turn to me, a mix of curiosity and anticipation evident in their gazes.

"Ladies and gentlemen," I nod, taking my seat at the head of the table. "Let's get started with our quarterly review."

For the next hour and a half, we dive into financial reports, marketing strategies, and projections for the upcoming quarter. I force myself to focus, pushing thoughts of Chase and Incendiary Ink to the back of my mind. But as Richard wraps up his financial summary, I know I can't put it off any longer.

"Before we adjourn," I say, my voice cutting through the rustling of papers, "there's one more matter we need to discuss."

The room grows quiet, all eyes on me once again.

"I received a call just before this meeting. Incendiary Ink is being inducted into the Rock and Roll Hall of Fame." I pause, letting the information sink in. "And apparently, they want me to give the induction speech."

The room erupts in excited chatter. Incendiary Ink had been one of Blackmore Records' most significant success stories, and their induction is a feather in the company's cap.

"That's fantastic news, Eliza!" exclaims Tom, already no doubt planning PR strategies in his head.

He's been filling in for our VP of Public Relations, Tess, who is currently on maternity leave. "Think of the publicity—"

I hold up a hand, silencing him. "It's not that simple, Tom. The induction speech is typically given by a musical peer, or an actor or celebrity of some kind, not a label exec."

"But you're not just any label exec," interjects Bess, her curly red hair bouncing as she leans forward enthusiastically. "You discovered them, nurtured them. Hell, you practically midwifed their career. And so many others, too. You're a legend in your own right."

My lips quirk in a sardonic smile. If only they knew just how involved I'd been in Incendiary Ink's journey. Late-night studio sessions, heated arguments over creative direction, stolen moments in hotel rooms with Chase...

"Be that as it may," I continue, pushing the memories aside, "it's unprecedented. And… complicated."

Cassidy Townsend, our head of legal, leans forward, her sharp blue eyes narrowing. "Complicated how, Eliza? From a legal standpoint, I don't see any issues. Our contract with them is over, but that doesn't preclude you from participating in the ceremony."

I resist the urge to roll my eyes. Of course, Cassidy would see it that way. As the wife of Jake Townsend, lead singer of Murderous Crows, another of our top-selling bands, she's used to the blurred

5

lines between business and personal lives in the music industry.

"It's not about legalities, Cassidy," I say, trying to keep the exasperation out of my voice. "It's about optics. Our relationship with Incendiary Ink wasn't exactly smooth sailing towards the end. Do we really want to dredge all that up again?"

The room grows quiet. Everyone remembers the scandals, rehab stints, and explosive arguments that occasionally spilled into the public eye.

Cassidy's lips twitch into a knowing smirk. "Sometimes, Eliza, dredging up the past is exactly what's needed to move forward. Look at Jake and me - we've weathered our share of storms, and Murderous Crows are stronger for it."

I bristle at the comparison. Cassidy might think she understands, but she has no idea about the complexity of my history with Chase and Incendiary Ink.

"With all due respect, Eliza," Richard chimes in, "I think you're letting personal feelings cloud your judgment here. This could be a huge opportunity for the label."

Before I can retort, a familiar voice cuts through the tension.

"Mom, you can't be serious."

My head snaps up. My son, Justin, stands in the doorway, a knowing smirk on his face. At thirty, he's the spitting image of his father—my first ex-husband —but with my steel grey eyes.

"Justin, what are you doing here? This is a closed meeting."

He shrugs, unrepentant. "Jenna let me in. Said it was important." He strolls into the room, perching on the edge of the conference table. "You have to do this, Mom. It's Incendiary Ink. It's Chase."

The name sends another jolt through my system. I keep my face impassive, but inside, a storm is brewing. Chase Avery. The one that got away. The man who has simultaneously been my greatest professional triumph and my most profound personal regret.

"I don't have to do anything," I reply, my tone clipped.

Justin leans in, his voice low enough that only I can hear. "You've been burying yourself in work since their farewell tour. Maybe it's time to face the music, don't you think?"

I glare at my son, but there's no real heat behind it. He knows me too well, damn him.

I turn back to the board, all of whom are watching the exchange with varying degrees of interest. "I'll think about it. That's all I can promise for now. I must let the Rock Hall know by the end of the week, so you'll know when they know. Meeting adjourned."

As the board members file out, chattering excitedly among themselves, I remain seated, lost in thought. Justin squeezes my shoulder as he passes.

"For what it's worth," he says softly, "I think it's about time you and Chase figured your shit out."

With that parting shot, he's gone, leaving me alone with my thoughts and a decision that threatens to upend the careful balance I've maintained for years.

Chase Avery. Incendiary Ink. The Hall of Fame.

"Well, fuck," I mutter to the empty room. I have a feeling my life is about to get a lot more complicated.

March 10, 2004

The thrum of bass vibrates through the soles of my Manolo Blahniks as I push through the doors of The Viper Room. At thirty-five, I feel almost ancient amid the sea of twenty-somethings, but I straighten my shoulders and lift my chin. I'm Eliza fucking Kerr, the youngest head of A&R in Blackmore Records' history, and I'm here to do my job.

I check my flip phone one last time before tucking it back into my purse. No messages from Mrs. Goldstein, Justin's babysitter. I push down the familiar pang of guilt. Eight-year-olds should be tucked in by their mothers, not paid caregivers. But this is my reality – single mom by day, talent scout by night.

The smell of stale beer, cigarette smoke, and a hint of something less legal assaults my senses. It's a far cry from the sterile, air-conditioned offices I left an hour ago, where I was negotiating a multi-million dollar contract renewal. But this – this grimy, pulsing underbelly of the music world – this is where the magic happens. It's also where dreams shatter, and hearts break. I should know; I've been on both sides of that equation. Rising stars can't always handle the heat, and shooting stars burn out. This business isn't easy for anyone. Not everyone can handle the pressure involved in being a success.

I scan the dimly lit room, my steel-grey eyes adjusting to the darkness. The crowd is a mix of industry types like myself, trying hard to look casual in their designer jeans and vintage band tees, and the genuine article – young, hungry music lovers with an edge that can't be bought at Barneys.

A flash of copper catches my eye. "Eliza! Over here!"

I spot Bess, my assistant, waving frantically from a table near the stage. Her wild red curls are impossible to miss, even in this lighting. I navigate my way over, nodding to a few familiar faces as I pass. Jerry from Sony, Mick from Universal – we're all here for the same reason. The hunt for the next big thing.

"You made it!" Bess grins, practically bouncing in her seat. At twenty-four, she's closer in age to the crowd around us, but her enthusiasm makes her seem even younger. "I was worried you might bail for that charity gala everyone wanted a ticket to."

I slide into the seat beside her, signaling the waitress for a drink. "And miss the chance to see the band you've been raving about for weeks? Not a chance." I don't mention that I've already been to three shows this week, each one a disappointment. In this industry, you have to kiss a lot of frogs before you find a prince.

"Trust me, they're worth it. Incendiary Ink is going to blow you away."

I raise an eyebrow, accepting a glass of overpriced white wine from the waitress. "Big words, Bess. Let's hope they live up to the hype." I take a sip, savoring the crisp taste. It's my one indulgence tonight; I need to keep a clear head.

"Just wait until you see and hear the lead singer, Chase Avery. Then you'll get it."

My internal cynicism smirks. "If you say so…"

As the lights dim further, I feel a familiar surge of anticipation, tinged with a hint of something else. Wariness, perhaps. Or maybe it's just the echo of a lesson learned the hard way. The last time I felt this excited about a new act, it ended with a gold band on my finger and a crying baby in my arms. Don't get me wrong – Justin is the best thing that ever happened to me. But his father? Let's just say mixing business with pleasure in this industry rarely ends well.

The band takes the stage without fanfare, no dramatic entrance, or flashy effects. Just three guys with their instruments, looking for all the world like they've just rolled out of bed and onto the stage. But then the lead singer steps up to the mic, and I feel the air leave my lungs.

He's beautiful in that disheveled, rock-and-roll way that is infuriating and irresistible. Dark hair falls in his eyes, which are lined with just a hint of smudged kohl. His lean body is clad in torn jeans and a faded t-shirt that's seen better days. But it's his presence that captivates – an effortless charisma that draws all eyes to him.

I've seen a thousand singers just like him. I've signed a few, and broken the hearts of many more. I've learned the hard way not to mix business with pleasure, no matter how attractive the package. The diamond-less ring finger on my left hand is a constant reminder of that particular life lesson.

And then he starts to sing.

His voice cuts through my cynicism like a hot knife through butter. It's raw and powerful, with an emotional depth that belies his young age. The lyrics are sharp and clever, cutting through the noise with a clarity that's rare in the current music scene.

I find myself leaning forward, completely engrossed. For the first time in years, I feel that spark, that excitement that drew me to this industry in the first place. It's the same feeling that led me to Justin's father all those years ago. The thought should be a bucket of cold water, but somehow, it's not enough to douse the heat building inside me.

As the set progresses, I watch the other members too. The drummer, a big guy with arms like tree trunks, plays with an almost alarming ferocity. The tall guitarist, lanky with a shock of bright blue hair, provides a steady counterpoint to the lead singer's energy.

But it's the singer who plays bass so expertly, but it feels like an afterthought – Chase, if the screams from the audience are anything to go by – who holds my attention. There's something about him, a star quality that can't be manufactured or faked. The same quality made me fall for Justin's dad, but there's something different here. Something more.

I know I'm witnessing something special by the time they finish their set with a haunting ballad. The room erupts into thunderous applause, and I'm on my feet before I realize it, clapping along with everyone else.

I turn to Bess, not bothering to hide my excitement. "Find out everything you can about them. I'm going to try to get a meeting set up for tomorrow."

She grins, already tapping away on her Blackberry. "I told you they were good."

"Good doesn't begin to cover it," I mutter, my eyes still fixed on the stage where the band is packing up their gear.

As I move through the crowd towards them, I can already hear the opening lines of my pitch forming in my head. But underneath the professional excitement, there's something else. A flutter in my stomach that has nothing to do with business and everything to do with the way Chase's t-shirt clings to his lean frame as he bends to pack up his guitar.

I push the feeling aside. I'm here to sign a fucking band, not to fall for a pretty face and a voice that makes my knees weak. I've been down that road before, and I have the emotional scars and a precocious eight-year-old to show for it.

But as Chase looks up and our eyes meet, I have a feeling things aren't going to be that simple. Not this time. And despite every hard-learned lesson, every late night with a crying baby, every bitter argument with my ex, I can't bring myself to look away.

God help me. I think I'm in trouble.

As I approach the stage, I square my shoulders and put on my most professional smile. Up close, the band looks even younger, barely out of their twenties. The blue-haired guitarist notices me first, nudging the drummer, who's busy breaking down his kit.

"Can we help you?" the guitarist asks, a hint of wariness in his voice.

"I hope so," I reply, pulling out my business card. "Eliza Kerr, Head of A&R at Blackmore Records. I'd love to set up a meeting with you guys."

Their eyes widen at the mention of Blackmore. It's a reaction I'm used to – we're not the biggest label out there, but we have a reputation for nurturing unique talent.

"Seriously?" The drummer abandons his cymbals, moving closer. "That would be amazing, right Chase?"

And there he is. The lead singer turns, and I find myself staring into eyes so green they put emeralds to shame. Up close, he's even more striking – all sharp cheekbones and full lips curved into a crooked smile.

"Chase Avery," he says, extending his hand. Even speaking, his voice has a musicality that sends a shiver down my spine. "These are Will and Mark. It's a pleasure to meet you, Ms. Kerr."

I take his hand, and it's like touching a live wire. There's a spark, an undeniable pull that catches me off guard. His hand is calloused from guitar strings, warm and strong around mine. For a moment, I forget to breathe.

"Eliza, please," I manage, withdrawing my hand perhaps a bit too quickly. "That was quite a performance. You guys have something special."

Chase's smile widens, revealing a dimple in his left cheek that should be illegal. "We like to think so. But it's nice to hear it from someone in the industry."

There's a flirtatious edge to his tone that I pointedly ignore. I've been in this business long enough to know better than to fall for the talent. It's my number one rule. Well, it is now, anyway.

"Well, I'd like to discuss your future plans. Are you free tomorrow afternoon? Say, 2 PM at our offices?"

The guys exchange excited glances. "We'll be there," Chase answers for all of them. "Wouldn't miss it for the world."

I hand him my card, our fingers brushing again. I'm prepared for the spark this time, but it doesn't make it any less potent. "Great. Don't be late. And bring your demo, if you have one." My breath catches in my throat, and I can't help but stare into Chase's eyes. I can't seem to look away. I find myself saying, "You're either going to be the biggest band in the world or the biggest disaster I've ever seen."

He stares back at me and arches a brow, his dimple making an unwelcome appearance. "At least we'll be memorable."

"See you tomorrow," I mumble under my breath, forcing myself to look away and break our connection. My fingers are still sparking where they met his, and a shot of electricity winds down my spine.

As I turn to leave, I feel his eyes on me. I glance back over my shoulder, catching his gaze once more. A look in his eyes – part challenge, part invitation – sends a shiver through my entire body.

"Looking forward to it, Eliza," he calls after me, my name rolling off his tongue like a caress.

I manage a nod and head back to Bess, my heart pounding in a way it hasn't in years. Part of me is thrilled at the prospect of signing this talented band. But another part – the part I've kept locked away since my divorce – is terrified by the effect Chase Avery has on me.

As I collect Bess and head for the exit, my phone buzzes. It's a text from Mrs. Goldstein.

> MRS. GOLDSTEIN: Justin had a nightmare. Asking for you.

Reality crashes back in, and I'm grateful for it. I have responsibilities, a son who needs me. I can't afford to get caught up in green eyes and dimpled smiles.

But as I hail a cab, I can't help but think about tomorrow's meeting. About seeing Chase again.

I have a feeling Incendiary Ink will be more than just my next big signing. They might just be the band that changes everything.

Little do I know just how right I am.

Play The Game Tonight

CHASE

THE RELENTLESS CALIFORNIA sun pierces through the gaps in my blackout curtains, a stark reminder that another day has begun. I groan, rubbing the sleep from my eyes, my body a map of aches from yesterday's brutal workout. At forty-five, staying in shape for potential comeback tours is a full-time job in itself. Not that we're planning a comeback at the moment, but it's something we talk about occasionally. Better safe than sorry.

My feet hit the cool hardwood floor, and I instinctively reach for the bottle on my nightstand. Water, not whiskey. Old habits die hard, but new ones save lives.

As I pad to the kitchen, the house is quiet save for the distant crash of waves against the Malibu shore. The silence used to be deafening, a void I'd fill with parties, groupies, anything to drown out the thoughts in my head. Now, it's a comfort. A reminder of how far I've come.

My eyes drift to the wall above the fireplace where my platinum records hang, a timeline of Incendiary Ink's rise to fame. Next to them sits a simpler but infinitely more precious award: my five-year sobriety chip. I pick it up, its weight familiar in my palm. Five years. 1,826 days of fighting, of choosing life over oblivion. All because one woman refused to give up on me.

Eliza.

The coffee maker gurgles to life, filling the kitchen with the rich aroma of freshly ground beans. It's a small luxury but one I savor. In my former life, mornings were for nursing hangovers and popping pills. Now, it's protein shakes and coffee, fuel for songwriting sessions and meetings with my therapist.

I carry my mug out to the deck, the sea breeze tousling my salt-and-pepper hair. The view still takes my breath away – endless blue ocean meeting cloudless sky. It's the kind of vista I used to dream about when we were crammed in a van, playing any dive bar that would have us. Back when Eliza was just our manager, not the woman who would shape the course of my life in ways I'm still understanding.

My phone buzzes, and Will's name flashes on the screen. I smile, remembering our late-night call about the Hall of Fame induction. It still feels surreal, like a dream I'm afraid to wake up from.

"Morning, Will," I answer, voice still rough with sleep.

"Dude, have you seen the news?" Will's voice crackles with a mixture of excitement and anxiety that immediately sets me on edge.

"What news?"

"It's everywhere. Eliza was officially announced as our inductee for the Hall of Fame ceremony."

The world tilts on its axis. *Eliza.* The name alone sends a tidal wave of memories crashing over me. Stolen kisses in studio booths. Screaming matches in hotel rooms. Her steady hand on my back as I retched into toilet bowls in cities I can't even remember.

Eliza Kerr. The woman who saw something in us – in me – when we were nothing but a bunch of kids with more attitude than talent. The one who fought tooth and nail for our success, who weathered every storm with us. The person I called at 3 AM when the demons got too loud, knowing she'd always answer.

The woman I loved but could never commit to, no matter how much I wanted to.

"Chase? You still there?" Will's voice cuts through the fog of memories.

"Yeah, I'm here," I manage, my throat suddenly dry. "That's... that's good, right? It's what we wanted."

"You sure you're okay with this? I mean, it was your idea, but if you're having second thoughts..."

I close my eyes, and I'm instantly transported back to that night. The last time I saw her. It wasn't at our farewell tour like I'd told the guys. No, it was worse. Much worse.

I'd shown up at her place, higher than the notes I could no longer hit, a whirlwind of paranoia and misplaced anger. The look in her eyes – not fear, but a bone-deep weariness – haunts me still. I'd spewed venom, accusing her of things that made no sense even in my drug-addled mind.

And yet, the next morning, there she was. Calm and composed, but with a sadness in her eyes that cut through even my chemical haze. "Chase," she'd said, her voice gentle but firm, "it's time. You need help. Real help. And I can't be the one to give it to you anymore."

That was the moment I knew. The moment I realized how much I'd hurt her, how much I'd taken her for granted. It was also the moment I knew I loved her more than anything in this world. And that I didn't deserve her.

"No," I say finally, coming back to the present. "No, it has to be Eliza. There's no one else who knows us – knows me – like she does."

"If you're sure," Will says, skepticism clear in his voice.

"I'm sure." And I am. Because despite everything, despite the years and the hurt and the regrets, there's a part of me that never stopped hoping for a reason to see her again. To make things right.

After I hang up, I sit on the deck for a long time,

watching the waves crash against the shore. The Hall of Fame. Eliza. It's like the universe is conspiring to bring my past crashing into my present.

I consider reaching out to her. My thumb hovers over her contact in my phone – I've never had the heart to delete it. But what would I say? *'Hey, long time no see. Thanks for agreeing to induct us into the Hall of Fame. Sorry for being a colossal asshole and breaking your heart. Oh, and thanks for saving my life. Want to grab coffee?'*

Yeah, that'll go over well.

Instead, I do what I've always done when emotions get too big to handle. I grab my guitar – the same beat-up acoustic Eliza gifted me for my 30th birthday. As my fingers find the familiar chords, a melody starts to form. It's bittersweet and a little raw, like an old wound that's never quite healed.

For the first time in years, I let myself really remember Eliza. The way her eyes shined when she laughed at my bad jokes. How she'd absentmindedly twirl her hair when deep in thought, poring over contracts. The fierce glint in her eye when she went to bat for us with record execs. The gentle way she'd tend to me after I'd pushed myself too hard, on stage or off.

I think about how far I've come since those days. The battles I've fought, the demons I've faced. I'm not that reckless rockstar anymore, drowning my feelings in booze and drugs. I'm sober now, thanks to her. But seeing Eliza again? That might be the biggest test of my strength yet.

As the sun climbs higher in the sky, I write a song about second chances and the ones that got away. About love and regrets. About the long, hard road to redemption and the hope that maybe, just maybe, it's not too late to make things right.

I write a song about Eliza and the man I've become because of her, and in spite of her.

And as the final notes fade away, carried off by the ocean breeze, I realize something. I'm terrified of seeing her again, of facing our past. But I'm even more terrified of letting this chance slip away.

This time, I'm not going to run. This time, I'm going to face the music.

Because Eliza Kerr didn't just save my career all those years ago. She saved my life. And it's about damn time I thanked her for it.

I pick up my phone again, this time with purpose. I don't call Eliza – I'm not quite there yet. Instead, I dial my therapist's number. If I'm going to do this, if I'm going to face Eliza and all the emotions that come with her, I need to be prepared. I need to be strong.

As the phone rings, I look at my reflection in the window. The man staring back at me isn't perfect. He's scarred, he's flawed, but he's trying. He's sober. He's alive.

And for the first time in a long time, he's ready to

stop running from his past and start fighting for his future.

"Hey, Dr. Hendricks? It's Chase. I think I'm going to need an extra session this week. Something big is coming up, and I need to be ready."

As I talk to my therapist, I feel a sense of calm settle over me. Whatever happens with Eliza, whatever comes next, I know one thing for sure: I'm not the same man I was five years ago. And maybe, just maybe, that's enough to start making things right.

March 11, 2004

The Blackmore Records lobby reeks of ambition and expensive perfume. I shift in the stylish but uncomfortable leather chair, its cool surface a stark contrast to the sweat beading on my lower back. My borrowed dress shirt itches, a constant reminder that I don't belong in this world of polished marble and abstract art.

To my left, Will's leg bounces like he's auditioning for a new drummer position. Mark sits unnaturally still on my right, his usual energy coiled tight, ready to snap.

"If you don't stop that," I mutter to Will, "I'm going to throw up on your shoes."

Will's leg freezes mid-bounce. "Shit, sorry," he whispers back. "I feel like I'm about to jump out of my skin."

Mark leans in, his breath smelling of the mints he's been chomping on since we arrived. "Remember the plan. United front. No matter what they offer, we discuss it privately first. Got it?"

We nod, a trio of terrified soldiers preparing for battle. The thing is, I'm not sure if we're fighting against Blackmore or our own self-doubt.

A sharp click-click-click of heels against marble slices through the tension. My head snaps up, and suddenly, there she is. Eliza Kerr, larger than life and twice as daunting.

Christ on a cracker.

If I thought she was stunning in the dim light of the Viper Room, she's absolutely devastating in broad daylight. Her charcoal outfit is all clean lines and subtle curves, projecting an aura of power that makes my mouth go dry. Her platinum hair is pulled back, revealing a face that could launch a thousand ships – or sink them with a single raised eyebrow.

But it's her eyes that hold me captive. Steel grey, sharp as a blade, and focused entirely on us. I feel laid bare, like she can see every dream, every fear, every half-formed lyric scribbled on bar napkins at 2 AM.

"Gentlemen," she says, her voice a low, rich timbre that settles somewhere deep in my chest. "Thank you for coming. Follow me, please."

24

As we trail after her, I can't help but notice every head turn as she passes. She's like a shark cutting through water, sleek, dangerous, and impossible to ignore. I'm both terrified and exhilarated by the thought of working with her.

The conference room is bigger than our entire practice space, with views of the LA skyline that remind me just how high the stakes are. Eliza gestures for us to sit, taking her place at the head of the table like a queen holding court.

"So," she begins, folding her hands in front of her. "Incendiary Ink. Let's talk about your future."

What follows is the most intense hour of my life. Eliza doesn't just ask questions; she dissects our answers, challenging every assumption, pushing us to think bigger, dream harder. She's not interested in what we think she wants to hear. She wants the truth, raw and unfiltered.

I find myself leaning forward, drawn into a verbal sparring match that's equal parts thrilling and terrifying. There's a glint in her eye when I push back against one of her points, a quirk of her lips when I make a particularly passionate argument about our sound. It's intoxicating.

Finally, she leans back, a chess master who's seen all the moves. "Alright, here's what Blackmore can offer you."

The deal she outlines is beyond our wildest dreams. Creative control, marketing budgets that make my head spin, and tour support that could put us in venues we've only dreamed of playing. It's more than we ever dared hope for, and I can feel the excitement building in the room.

As Eliza finishes laying out the offer, I glance at Will and Mark. Their faces mirror what I'm feeling - pure, unadulterated shock. We're stunned into silence, the magnitude of what's being offered rendering us momentarily speechless.

But Eliza misreads our silence. I watch as a flicker of uncertainty crosses her face, quickly replaced by determination. She leans forward, her eyes intense.

"I can see you're not convinced," she says, her voice taking on an edge of... is that desperation? No, that's not quite it. It's more like fierce determination. "So let me sweeten the deal."

We exchange confused glances. Sweeten the deal? How could it possibly get better than this?

Eliza takes a deep breath, and I can almost see the wheels turning in her head. She's making a decision right here, right now.

"I'll personally manage your band."

The words hang in the air, adding another layer of shock to our already overwhelmed minds. Did she just say what I think she said?

"You... what?" Will manages to croak out, his voice barely above a whisper.

Eliza nods, seeming to gain confidence as she

speaks. "You heard me. I'll be your manager. Direct access to me, 24/7. My full attention, my connections, my expertise - all at your disposal."

Mark's brow furrows. "But... you're the head of A&R. Can you even do that?"

"I can, and I will," Eliza says firmly. "If that's what it takes to sign Incendiary Ink to Blackmore, then that's what I'll do." She stands up, smoothing down her jacket. "I'll give you some time to discuss this. Take all the time you need."

As soon as the door closes behind her, we explode into a frenzy of whispered exclamations.

"Holy shit," Will hisses, eyes wide. "Did that just happen?"

Mark shakes his head in disbelief. "She wants to manage us personally. The head of A&R. This is insane."

I'm still trying to wrap my head around it all. "Guys, do you realize what this means? She's not just offering us a contract. She's investing herself in us. Personally."

"But why?" Will asks. "Why would she go to such lengths?"

I think about how Eliza's eyes lit up when she heard our demo, and the passion in her voice as she talked about our potential. "Because she believes in us. Really believes in us."

Mark nods slowly. "This could be huge for us.

Her connections, her experience... it could fast-track us in ways we've only dreamed of."

"But it's also a risk," Will points out. "What if it doesn't work out? What if we're not what she thinks we are?"

I lean back, running a hand through my hair. "Guys, think about it. She's putting her reputation on the line for us. This isn't just a business decision for her. This is personal."

We fall silent for a moment, the weight of the opportunity before us sinking in.

"So," Mark says finally. "What do we do?"

I look at each of them in turn, seeing the same mix of excitement and apprehension I'm feeling reflected in their eyes. "Sony and Universal were there last night too, and we haven't heard shit from them, right? I say we take the leap. This is our shot. Let's grab it with both hands."

Will grins, his earlier nervousness morphing into determination. "Hell yeah. Let's do this."

Mark nods, a slow smile spreading across his face. "Incendiary Ink, managed by Eliza Kerr. Has a nice ring to it."

When Eliza returns, we try to play it cool, but I'm pretty sure the grins splitting our faces give us away.

"We accept," I tell her, standing to shake her hand. "All of it. The deal, the management offer. We're in."

The smile that breaks across Eliza's face is radiant, a stark contrast to her usually composed demeanor. It's a smile that lights up her entire face, reaches her eyes, and does funny things to my insides.

"Well then," she says, her hand warm in mine. "Gentlemen, welcome to Blackmore Records. Let's make history."

As we shake hands, sealing the deal that will change our lives forever, I'm hit with the overwhelming feeling that this is just the beginning. Eliza Kerr has stormed into our lives like a force of nature, and I have a feeling nothing will ever be the same again.

Shouldn't Be With Me

ELIZA

THE LOS ANGELES skyline glitters beyond my office window, contrasting with the turmoil churning inside me. I've been staring at the same paragraph of the Hall of Fame induction guidelines for the past hour, the words blurring into meaningless shapes. *What the hell was I thinking, agreeing to do this?*

With a sigh, I push away from my desk and move to the small bar in the corner of my office. My hand hovers over the whiskey decanter – a relic from easier times – before settling on the sparkling water. As much as I'd like to soften the edges of my psyche right now, I have to keep my thoughts clear. Well, as clear as they can be with the vortex of emotions running through me anyway.

As I sip the cold drink, my eyes drift to the platinum records adorning my walls. Incendiary Ink's debut album. Their breakthrough third record. The farewell tour compilation. Each one is a testament to what we achieved together. Each one a reminder of what we lost.

What I've lost.

My phone buzzes, Justin's name flashing on the screen. I smile despite myself. My son, always checking in at the right moment.

"Hey, sweetheart," I answer, my voice softer than it's been all day.

"Mom, how are you holding up? Any regrets about saying yes to the induction speech?"

I pause, choosing my words carefully. "It's... complicated. But it's done now."

"Are you okay with this? Really?"

Am I? The question echoes in my mind, stirring up a whirlwind of emotions I've kept bottled up for five long years.

"I'm fine, Justin," I lie, my tone more clipped than I intended. "It's just a lot to prepare for."

"Mom," his voice softens, "I know there's history there. If you need to talk..."

"I appreciate that, honey, but I've got this under control." Even as I say the words, I know they're not true. But some burdens aren't meant for our children to bear.

After reassuring Justin and ending the call, I find myself drawn to the old filing cabinet in the corner of my office. With trembling hands, I pull open the bottom drawer and extract a worn leather journal.

I have boxes of mementos I've kept over my career, but it's been years since I've looked at this particular one. Years since I've allowed myself to revisit the memories contained within its pages. But now, with the weight of my decision pressing down on me, I feel compelled to confront the past.

I open the journal, and a photo slips out. It's from one of Incendiary Ink's early tours. There's Chase, young and vibrant, his arm slung casually around my shoulders. We're both laughing at something off-camera, caught in a moment of pure, unguarded joy.

My fingers trace the outlines of our faces, and I'm hit with a wave of nostalgia so strong it nearly knocks me off my feet. God, we were young. So full of hope and ambition. When did it all get so complicated?

As I flip through the pages, snippets of our shared history flash before my eyes. Late-night songwriting sessions. Heated arguments over creative directions. Stolen moments of tenderness in the back of tour buses and anonymous hotel rooms. The slow, painful unraveling of whatever it was we had.

And through it all, the music. Always the music.

I close the journal, feeling the weight of unre-solved emotions and unanswered questions. Why didn't he ever reach out? Did I mean so little to him in the end? Five years of silence. Five years of wondering, of second-guessing every decision, every moment we shared.

The hurt I've been suppressing bubbles to the surface, sharp and raw. I thought... I don't know what I thought. That maybe once he got clean, he'd reach out. That our history meant something. But nothing. Radio silence.

My eyes fall on my desk phone, and I'm seized by a sudden, reckless impulse. Before I can talk myself out of it, I'm dialing a number I know by heart despite years of disuse. It rings once, twice, three times. Just as I'm about to lose my nerve, there's a click.

"Eliza?" Chase's voice, deeper and raspier than I remember, sends a shiver down my spine.

I take a deep breath, steeling myself. "Chase. We need to talk about this induction ceremony."

There's a pause, pregnant with unspoken words and shared history. Then, "Yeah, I guess we do."

As I settle into my chair, my heart racing, I'm struck by a powerful sense of déjà vu. This nervousness, this electric anticipation tinged with fear – I've felt this before. Twenty years ago, in a dimly lit studio, when Chase and I crossed that line from professional to personal for the first time.

I remember how my hands shook as I reached for him, how my voice trembled when I whispered his name. The exhilaration and terror of stepping into unknown territory, of risking everything for a chance at something extraordinary.

Now, as I clear my throat to speak, I realize I'm standing on the edge of another precipice. The stakes are different, the terrain has changed, but that feeling – that mix of fear and hope and possibility – it's exactly the same.

"So," I begin, my voice steadier than I feel, "where should we start?"

As Chase begins to speak, I close my eyes and let myself be transported back to that night twenty years ago when everything changed. For better or worse, we're about to embark on another journey together. And just like then, I have no idea where it will lead us.

But this time, I'm older. Wiser. More guarded. This time, I tell myself, I won't let my heart get ahead of my head.

Even as I think it, though, a small voice in the back of my mind whispers a traitorous thought: Who am I kidding? When it comes to Chase Avery, my heart has always had a mind of its own.

May 15, 2004

The acrid smell of stale coffee and cigarettes hangs heavy in the air as I check my watch for the hundredth time. 2:37 AM. The studio's soundproofed walls can't quite muffle the muted thrum of the city outside, a constant reminder of the world beyond this cocoon of creativity and tension.

Joe, our sound engineer, hunches over the mixing board, his fingers dancing across faders and knobs with practiced precision. Beside him, Raphael, the producer Blackmore insisted on, nods along to a rhythm only he can hear. We've been at this for fourteen hours straight, but Chase had been adamant about nailing this track tonight.

I suppress a yawn, acutely aware of the mountain of paperwork waiting for me back at the office. Tour logistics, contract negotiations, press junkets – the never-ending demands of managing a band on the cusp of stardom. But right now, all of that fades into the background as I focus on the figure behind the glass.

Chase stands in the recording booth, headphones askew, a fine sheen of sweat glistening on his brow under the harsh studio lights. He's been wrestling with this song for days, chasing a perfection that seems just out of reach. The rest of the band – Will and Mark –left hours ago, frustration etched on their faces. But Chase... Chase couldn't let it go.

"One more take," I hear myself say, my voice hoarse from overuse and too much caffeine. "Let's try it one more time."

Joe and Raphael exchange a look I pretend not to see. I know we're pushing it, know that fatigue can be the enemy of creativity. But there's something in Chase's eyes, a fire that tells me we're close to something special.

Chase nods, determination etched on his face. He adjusts his headphones, closes his eyes, and as the backing track starts, he begins to sing.

The opening notes wash over me, and just like that, all my exhaustion melts away. His voice fills the studio, raw and powerful and achingly vulnerable. It's a sound that's been haunting my dreams for the past two months, ever since that night at the Viper Room. But this... this is something else entirely.

I find myself holding my breath, afraid to move lest I break the spell. The lyrics paint a vivid picture of longing and missed connections, of two people orbiting each other but never quite touching. As I listen, I can't shake the feeling that he's singing about us.

Which is ridiculous, of course. We're colleagues. I'm his manager, for God's sake. Whatever tension exists between us is purely professional. It has to be. The industry is littered with cautionary tales of managers who crossed that line, who let their personal feelings cloud their judgment. I've worked too hard, climbed too high, to risk it all for... what? A fleeting attraction?

But as Chase's voice soars into the bridge, raw emotion bleeding through every word, I feel my carefully constructed walls beginning to crumble.

The song ends, the last note hanging in the air like a question. For a moment, none of us moves. Then Chase opens his eyes, meeting my gaze through the glass. The intensity I see there makes my heart skip a beat.

"How was that?" he asks over the talkback mic, a hint of vulnerability creeping into his voice.

I look to Joe and Raphael. Joe gives an approving nod, while Raphael leans back, a satisfied smirk playing on his lips.

"It was perfect, Chase," I say, trying to keep my voice steady. "I think we've got it."

He grins, that boyish smile that never fails to make my stomach flip. "Great. Let's hear it back."

As Joe queues up the playback, Chase joins us in the control room. He stands close – too close – as we listen, his arm brushing against mine. I can feel the heat radiating off him, smell the faint scent of his cologne mixed with sweat and coffee. It's intoxicating.

The song ends, and we stand in silence for a moment, all processing what we've just created.

"That's a wrap, folks," Joe announces, stretching. "Great session. I'll start the mixdown tomorrow... or I guess later today."

Raphael claps Chase on the back. "Kid, I think you just wrote yourself a hit. This could be the one that breaks you wide open."

As Joe and Raphael begin shutting down the

equipment, trading technical jargon I only half understand, Chase turns to me. "Eliza," he says softly. "I think we've just made something special."

I nod, not trusting myself to speak. Because he's right – the song is incredible. But more than that, I'm acutely aware of how close we're standing, of the electricity crackling in the air between us.

"We make a good team," I manage to say, aiming for a light, professional tone.

Chase doesn't answer immediately. Instead, he glances at Joe and Raphael, then back to me. "Can we talk? Privately?"

My heart races as I nod, following Chase out of the control room and into the small kitchenette down the hall. As soon as the door closes behind us, the air seems to thicken with unspoken words and suppressed desires.

"Chase," I start, a warning and a question all at once.

"I know," he says, his voice low. "I know all the reasons why we shouldn't. The band, the label, our careers. But Eliza... tell me you don't feel this too."

And in that moment, all my carefully constructed walls come crumbling down. Because I do feel it. I've been feeling it since the moment we met, trying to ignore it, to push it aside in the name of professionalism. But here, in the dim light of the kitchenette, with Chase looking at me like I'm the only person in the world, I can't deny it any longer.

I lean in, or maybe he does – I'm not sure. All I know is that suddenly we're kissing, and it's like every cliché I've ever rolled my eyes at. Fireworks. Sparks. The world falling away until there's nothing but this moment, this feeling. An arm wraps around my waist, and he pulls me closer while his other hand slides to the back of my neck, deepening the kiss.

This is heaven. This is a connection I've never felt before. And it scares the shit out of me.

When we finally break apart, we're both breathing heavily. Chase rests his forehead against mine, his eyes closed.

"We probably shouldn't have done that," I say, even as every fiber of my being screams for more.

Chase chuckles softly. "Probably not," he agrees. Then he opens his eyes, meeting my gaze with a seriousness that takes my breath away. "But I don't regret it. Do you?"

I should say yes. I should step back, reestablish professional boundaries, pretend this never happened. It's the smart thing to do, the safe thing. I think about Justin, about the responsibility I have to him, about the example I should be setting. I think about the band, about the delicate balance of personalities and egos I navigate daily. I think about my career, about all the sacrifices I've made to get where I am.

But looking into Chase's eyes, feeling the warmth of his embrace, all those concerns seem distant, manageable.

"No," I whisper. "I don't regret it. At least, not yet."

Chase's answering smile is radiant. He leans in to kiss me again, and as I melt into his embrace, a small voice in the back of my mind whispers a dire warning: *This is going to complicate everything.*

But with Chase's arms around me and the echo of that song still playing in my mind, I can't bring myself to care. Whatever complications may come, in this moment, everything feels perfectly, wonderfully right.

It was a kiss. Just a kiss. Well, not *just* a kiss. The most amazing kiss I've ever had. But something tells me it's the beginning of something unstoppable. Something dangerous. Something that feels amazing now but is going to destroy both of us later.

"I… should go," I say, forcing myself to pull away from him. It almost physically hurts. "Justin will be up soon for school."

His face falls, but he covers it quickly, his hands falling from my waist. I have to suppress a shudder at the chill from the loss of his warmth.

"Right," he says, a crooked smile showcasing his dimple. "To be continued."

My heart stutters at his words, and fear runs through me. Was this a giant mistake? Did I just ruin everything? Did I let my heart lead my head yet again? I should know better than to let this happen.

What about my rules? Aren't they there for a reason? What the fuck am I doing?

It was just a kiss.

As we leave the studio, the first hints of dawn streaking the sky, I can't shake the feeling that we've just set something monumental in motion. For better or worse, nothing will ever be the same again.

Sin on Skin

CHASE

"SO," Eliza's voice comes through the phone, crisp and professional. "Where should we start?"

My breath catches in my throat. Five years, and her voice still has the power to stop me in my tracks. I pace the length of my living room, bare feet silent on the polished hardwood, phone pressed to my ear. Outside, the Malibu surf crashes against the shore, a rhythmic counterpoint to my racing heart.

"How about we start with hello?" I say, aiming for lightness but hearing the tension in my own voice. "It's good to hear from you, Eliza."

There's a pause, heavy with unspoken words. I close my eyes, picturing her: the furrow between her brows as she weighs her words, the way she'd twirl a strand of hair around her finger when she was thinking. *Does she still do that?*

"Hello, Chase," she finally says, her tone softening almost imperceptibly. "I think we should discuss the logistics of the induction ceremony."

Of course. Straight to business. That's Eliza all over. But I can't just ignore the elephant in the room, the five years of silence between us. Five years of regret, of growth, of wondering 'what if?'

"Sure, we can talk logistics," I say, running a hand through my hair – longer now, streaked with silver. "But don't you think we should address the fact that this is the first time we've spoken in five years?"

I hear her sharp intake of breath. "Chase, I don't think-"

"Please, Eliza," I cut in, my voice low and urgent. "I know you want to keep this professional, but we can't just pretend like there isn't a history here."

Another pause, longer this time. I use it to steel myself, to remind myself that I'm not that reckless kid anymore. I'm sober now. Stable. The man she always believed I could be.

"Fine," she says finally, a hint of that familiar fire in her voice. "You want to talk about it? Let's talk. Why haven't you reached out in five years, Chase?"

The question hits me like a physical blow, even though I was expecting it. I sink onto my couch, the leather cool against my skin. My eyes fall on the five-year sobriety chip on my coffee table, a constant reminder of how far I've come – and who I have to thank for it.

"I... I wanted to," I begin, the words feeling inadequate. "God, Eliza, you have no idea how many times I picked up the phone, started to dial your number."

"But you didn't," she says, her voice tight with an emotion I can't quite place. Hurt? Anger? Both? "As a matter of fact, I believe you even blocked my number, which is why I'm calling from this phone."

"No, I didn't call. And…yes, I did," I admit, the shame of it washing over me anew. "I couldn't, Eliza. After everything I put you through, everything you did for me... I didn't know how to face you."

I think back to that last day I saw her, when she dropped me off at the final rehab, the way she looked at me – a mixture of hope and resignation that haunts me still. "I thought I was doing the right thing," I continue. "Giving you space, letting you move on with your life without me complicating things."

"That wasn't your decision to make, Chase," Eliza says, her professional facade cracking slightly. "Do you have any idea-" She stops abruptly, and I hear her take a deep breath. "Never mind. It doesn't matter now."

But it does matter. It matters more than anything. "I'm sorry, Eliza," I say, the words feeling wholly inadequate. "I know it's not enough, but I am. I've wanted to tell you that for five years."

There's a long silence, filled only by the sound of our breathing. I find myself holding my breath, waiting.

Finally, she sighs. "I appreciate that, Chase. But it

doesn't change anything. We have a job to do now, and we need to focus on that."

I want to argue, to tell her that it changes everything. That I'm not the same man I was five years ago, that I've grown, that I've never stopped thinking about her. That every song I've written since we met, even the ones no one's heard, are all about her. But I know Eliza. I know pushing her now will only make her retreat further.

"Okay," I say, swallowing my disappointment. "You're right. Let's talk about the ceremony."

As Eliza launches into a discussion about schedules and protocols, I listen with half an ear, my mind whirling. Her voice washes over me, bringing back a flood of memories: late-night strategy sessions, heated arguments over creative decisions, quiet moments of understanding when the world became too much.

She might want to keep things strictly professional, but I can't. Not when it comes to her. Not when there's still so much left unsaid between us.

The induction ceremony isn't just about celebrating our music. It's a second chance. A chance to make things right with Eliza, to show her the man I've become. And I'll be damned if I'm going to let it slip away.

As we wrap up the call, I find myself saying, "Eliza, wait."

"Yes?" Her voice is guarded, but I detect a hint

of... something. Curiosity? Hope? Maybe I'm just projecting my own hope onto her. It wouldn't be the first fucking time.

"I just wanted to say... I'm looking forward to seeing you. To working with you again." What I don't say: I've missed you. Every day. In ways I didn't even know were possible.

There's a pause, and when she speaks, her voice is softer than it's been the entire call. "I'm looking forward to it too, Chase. Goodnight."

The line goes dead, but I sit there for a long time, phone still pressed to my ear. Outside, the sun is setting, painting the sky in shades of pink and gold that Eliza would have loved. It's not much, but it's a start. A tiny crack in the wall she's built around herself. And I'm determined to find a way through, no matter how long it takes.

I stand, walking to my music room. My fingers itch to pick up a guitar, to channel these swirling emotions into song. Because some things are worth fighting for. And Eliza Kerr? She's always been worth everything.

As I start to play, a new melody forming under my fingers, I make a silent promise. This time, I won't let fear or cowardice hold me back. This time, I'll show Eliza the man I've become – the man she always saw in me.

This time, I'll get it right.

August 20, 2004

The rooftop bar of the Mondrian is a sea of beautiful people, all here to celebrate us. Incendiary Ink. The next big thing, if the music press is to be believed. Our debut album dropped last week, and it's already climbing the charts faster than anyone expected.

I should be on top of the world. Instead, I'm hiding in a corner, nursing a whiskey and searching the crowd for one face in particular.

Eliza.

She's been keeping her distance since that night in the studio, three months ago. That kiss... *God, that kiss*. It's been haunting my dreams, making my fingers itch to touch her again. But she's been all business since then – organizing interviews, negotiating deals, smoothing ruffled feathers when Will and Mark inevitably piss someone off. The easy camaraderie we had before, the lingering glances and "accidental" touches... that's all gone.

I get it. I do. What happened between us that night was a mistake. A beautiful, intoxicating mistake that I can't stop thinking about, but a mistake nonetheless. She made that clear the next day, all business-like efficiency as she laid out all the reasons why it couldn't happen again.

I agreed, of course. What else could I do? But that doesn't mean I've stopped wanting her. If anything, the enforced distance has only made my attraction stronger. Every time she walks into a room, it's like all the air gets sucked out. I find myself staring at the curve of her neck, the way her lips move when she talks, the subtle sway of her hips when she walks. It's driving me crazy.

"There you are!" Will's voice booms over the music. He slings an arm around my shoulders, clearly three sheets to the wind. "Dude, why are you hiding? This is our night!"

I paste on a smile. "Just taking it all in, man. It's surreal, you know?"

Will nods sagely, then his eyes light up. "Oh shit, there's that hottie from Rolling Stone. I'm gonna go see if she wants an... exclusive interview." He waggles his eyebrows suggestively before disappearing into the crowd.

I shake my head, chuckling. Same old Will. My amusement fades as I spot a flash of platinum blonde hair across the rooftop. Eliza. She's deep in conversation with some suit – probably from the label – but even from here, I can see the tension in her shoulders.

Before I can talk myself out of it, I'm moving through the crowd towards her. As I get closer, I catch snippets of their conversation.

"...need to get them back in the studio," the suit is saying. "Strike while the iron's hot. We can have another album out by spring."

Eliza's smile is polite, but I can see the steel in her eyes. "With all due respect, Mr. Daniels, I think that would be a mistake. The boys need to tour, build their fanbase, get some real-world experience under their belts. Rushing into a second album could-"

"Ms. Kerr," Daniels cuts her off, his tone patronizing. "I appreciate your... enthusiasm, but perhaps you should leave the big picture decisions to those of us with more experience. The market moves fast these days. We can't afford to wait."

I see Eliza's jaw clench, and something in me snaps. "Actually," I say, stepping up beside her, "I think we should listen to Eliza. She hasn't steered us wrong yet."

Daniels looks at me, surprised. "Chase, I didn't see you there."

"Clearly," I say, flashing him my most charming smile. "Now, if you'll excuse us, I need to borrow my manager for a moment. Band business, you understand."

Without waiting for a response, I guide Eliza away smoothly, my hand on the small of her back. The contact sends sparks shooting up my arm, and I have to resist the urge to pull her closer.

"Thanks for the save," she murmurs as we reach a

quieter corner of the rooftop. "But I had it under control."

"I know you did," I say, dropping my hand reluctantly. "I just couldn't stand watching that asshole talk down to you."

Eliza looks at me, really looks at me, for the first time in months. "Chase..."

"I miss you," I blurt out, the words escaping before I can stop them. "I miss us, Eliza. The way we were before... before that kiss."

She closes her eyes, pain flashing across her face. "We can't, Chase. You know we can't. There's too much at stake."

"I know, I know," I say quickly. "I'm not asking for... I don't know what I'm asking for." I run a hand through my hair, frustrated. "I just know that I can't keep pretending there's nothing between us."

Eliza is quiet for a long moment, her eyes searching mine. Then, to my surprise, she grabs my hand. "Come with me," she says, leading me towards the exit.

We end up in her hotel room, the door barely closed before we're kissing again with me holding her against the wall. It's even better than I remembered – hot and desperate and full of months of pent-up desire. My hands roam her body, memorizing every curve, as hers tangle in my hair.

When we finally break apart, we're both breathing

hard. "We really shouldn't be doing this," Eliza whispers, but she makes no move to pull away.

I rest my forehead against hers, my heart pounding. "Do you want to stop?"

Her eyes meet mine, dark with desire. "No," she breathes, and it's all the invitation I need.

I kiss her again, slower this time, savoring the taste of her. My hands find the zipper of her dress, and I pause, silently asking permission. Eliza nods, and I slowly lower the zipper, revealing smooth, pale skin that I've dreamed about for months.

The dress pools at her feet, and I take a step back, drinking in the sight of her. "God, Eliza," I murmur. "You're beautiful."

A blush creeps across her cheeks, and it's so endearing that I have to kiss her again. Her hands find the buttons of my shirt, deftly undoing them. I shrug it off, then pull her close, reveling in the feeling of skin against skin.

We move towards the bed, a tangle of limbs and heated kisses. I lay her down gently, hovering over her, still hardly believing this is real. "Are you sure?" I ask, needing to hear her say it.

Eliza's hand comes up to cup my cheek. "I'm sure, Chase," she says softly. "I want this. I want you."

Those words ignite something in me, and I capture her lips in a searing kiss. We take our time exploring each other's bodies, hands and lips mapping out new territories. Every sigh, every shiver, every soft moan is etched into my memory.

When we finally come together, it's with a sense of inevitability, like two puzzle pieces clicking into place. We move together in perfect synchronicity, as if we've done this a thousand times before. I lose myself in the feeling of her, in the sound of her breath catching, in the way she says my name like a prayer.

Afterwards, we lie tangled in the sheets, my fingers tracing lazy patterns on her skin. I feel more relaxed, more content than I have in years. But as the afterglow fades, I can sense Eliza withdrawing, see the walls going back up behind her eyes.

"This can't happen again," she says, but there's no conviction in her voice. There's something in her posture that makes me think she means it, though. It's as if she's fighting a war inside herself over me, and I'm losing.

I can't lose this. Not now.

I prop myself up on an elbow, looking down at her. "What if... what if we made a rule?" The idea forms as I speak. "No strings attached. Just this, when we both want it. No expectations, no complications."

Eliza raises an eyebrow. "No strings attached? You really think we can do that?"

I shrug, trying to sound more confident than I feel. It's the only thing I could think of off the top of my head to keep her close to me. I don't want to lose her, and I'll take whatever I can get at this point. "Why not? We're both adults. We can keep it casual, right?"

She studies me for a long moment, then nods slowly. "Okay. No strings attached. And nobody can know about this. But Chase, the moment it starts to affect the band, or your career-"

"It won't," I promise, sealing it with a soft kiss. "Trust me, Eliza. I've got this under control."

As I pull her close again, a small voice in the back of my mind whispers a warning. One I should probably listen to, but it's not loud enough to drown out the emotions running through me at the moment. So, I ignore it, too caught up in the intoxicating feeling of having Eliza in my arms.

No strings attached. I can do that. I can totally do that.

Sucker.

Hell You Call A Dream

ELIZA

THE SCENT of Chanel No. 5 fills the air as I spritz it on my wrists, a comforting ritual that does little to calm my nerves tonight. I stare at my reflection in the full-length mirror, smoothing down the front of my black Armani cocktail dress. It's elegant, professional – armor for the battle ahead. But as I fasten the clasp of my mother's vintage pearl necklace, my hands are shaking. It's a bit formal for me, but it feels like armor. And I definitely feel like I need some sort of protection tonight.

What the hell was I thinking, agreeing to have dinner with Chase?

The phone call had been difficult enough. Hearing his voice after five years of silence brought back a flood of memories – both sweet and painful. And now I've agreed to see him face to face, to sit across a table from him and discuss the Hall of

Fame induction as if we're nothing more than old colleagues.

I close my eyes, taking a deep breath. I can do this. I'm Eliza fucking Kerr. I've negotiated million-dollar deals, managed impossible egos, navigated the treacherous waters of the music industry for decades. Just last week, I talked down a temperamental rapper from walking out mid-tour over a dispute about his rider. I can handle one dinner with Chase Avery.

But even as I think it, I know it's a lie. Because Chase was never just another musician, another client. He was... *everything*. And that's exactly why I shouldn't go tonight.

A soft knock at my bedroom door interrupts my spiraling thoughts. "Mom?" Justin's voice calls out. "You okay in there?"

I open the door to find my son leaning against the frame, concern etched on his face. "I'm fine, honey," I say, forcing a smile. "Just... nervous about this dinner."

Justin raises an eyebrow, so much like me it's almost comical. "You know, you don't have to go if you're not ready."

For a moment, I'm tempted to take the out he's offering. But I shake my head. "No, I need to do this. For the band, for the label... for me."

He nods, understanding in his eyes. Sometimes I forget how much he's seen. How much he's been through with me and the band. "Well, if you need an excuse to bail early, just text me. I'll call with a family emergency."

I laugh, some of the tension easing from my shoulders. "My hero," I say, reaching up to ruffle his hair like I did when he was little. He ducks away, grinning.

As Justin heads back to his room – he's been staying with me while his place is being renovated – I turn back to the mirror. The woman staring back at me is successful, respected, powerful. But I can see the vulnerability in her eyes, the fear.

Before I can talk myself out of it, I grab my phone and dial a familiar number.

"Eliza?" Michelle's voice comes through, warm and slightly concerned. "Everything okay?"

I sink onto the edge of my bed, tension easing from my shoulders at the sound of my best friend's voice. "I'm not sure, Michelle. I think I might be making a huge mistake."

Michelle Reeves has been my right hand at Blackmore for the past decade, rising from my assistant to become our Vice President. Along the way she's become one of my best friends. Someone I can trust. She's one of the few people who knows the full story of my history with Chase.

"Is this about the dinner with Chase?" she asks, cutting straight to the heart of the matter as always.

"How did you know?"

I can almost hear her eye roll through the phone.

"Please. You've been on edge ever since you agreed to do the induction speech. It doesn't take a genius to figure out why. Plus, you kinda still share your calendar with me, so…"

I sigh, twisting a strand of hair around my finger. "I don't know if I can do this, Michelle. Seeing him again, after everything..."

"Hey," Michelle's voice softens. "You're one of the strongest people I know, Eliza. You've dealt with far worse than an awkward dinner with an ex. Remember when we had to renegotiate all our streaming contracts after that royalty dispute last year?"

I chuckle despite myself. "God, don't remind me. I still have nightmares about spreadsheets and fine print."

"And you handled it like the boss bitch you are," Michelle says. "You can handle this too."

I stand, pacing the length of my bedroom. The plush carpet muffles my footsteps, a counterpoint to the clicking of my heels that usually accompanies my movements at the office. "He's not just an ex, Michelle," I say softly. "You know that."

"I know," she says gently. "But that's exactly why you need to do this. You need closure, Eliza. And who knows? Maybe this is your chance to finally get some answers."

"Or maybe it's a chance to reopen old wounds," I counter, pausing to look out the window at the twinkling Los Angeles skyline. "God, Michelle, you didn't see him at the end. The things he said, the way he looked at me... like I was the enemy."

"That was five years ago," Michelle reminds me. "People change. You've changed. Hell, you're about to induct Incendiary Ink into the freaking Hall of Fame. If that's not a full-circle moment, I don't know what is."

She's right, of course. But that doesn't make this any easier.

"What if..." I start, then stop, the words sticking in my throat as if I'm afraid to put them out into the universe again.

"What if what?" Michelle prompts.

"What if I still have feelings for him?" The admission hangs in the air, heavy with implications.

There's a pause on the other end of the line. Then, "Oh, honey. I think we both know you never stopped having feelings for him. The question is, what are you going to do about it?"

I look at myself in the mirror again, really look. Beyond the designer dress and the carefully applied makeup, I see the woman who fell in love with a young rocker against her better judgment. The woman who helped build Incendiary Ink into a global phenomenon, only to watch it all crumble. The woman who's spent five years trying to forget the one man she can't seem to let go of.

"I don't know," I admit. "But I guess I have to go to this dinner to find out."

"That's my girl," Michelle says, and I can hear the smile in her voice. "Now, go knock him dead. And Eliza?"

"Yeah?"

"Remember – you're Eliza fucking Kerr. You've got this."

I hang up, feeling slightly more centered. Michelle's right. I am Eliza fucking Kerr. I've faced down record execs, diva artists, and cutthroat competitors. I can handle one dinner with Chase Avery. Maybe if I keep repeating that mantra in my head, I'll eventually believe it.

Maybe.

But as I grab my Hermès clutch and head for the door, a small voice in the back of my mind whispers a warning: *This isn't just any dinner. This is Chase.* And when it comes to him, all bets are off.

"I'm heading out," I call to Justin. "Don't wait up."

"Good luck, Mom," he calls back. "Remember, family emergency is just a text away."

I smile, grateful for my son's support. Then, taking a deep breath, I step out into the warm Los Angeles night.

Here goes nothing.

February 14, 2005

The last thing I expect to see when I walk into my hotel room is a heart-shaped box of chocolates and a bouquet of red roses on the bed. For a moment, my heart leaps – then reality crashes back in. This isn't for me. It can't be.

I grab my phone, firing off a quick text to Chase.

> ME: Wrong room?

His reply comes almost instantly.

> CHASE: Nope. Happy Valentine's Day, Eliza.

I stare at the message, a mix of emotions swirling in my chest. Anger. Confusion. And something dangerously close to hope. Before I can stop myself, I'm dialing his number.

"Hey," Chase's voice is warm, a little uncertain. "Did you get the-"

"What the hell are you doing?" I cut him off, my voice sharper than I intend.

There's a pause. "I... I thought it would be nice. To do something for Valentine's Day."

I close my eyes, pinching the bridge of my

nose. "Chase, we agreed. No strings attached, remember? This," I gesture at the gifts even though he can't see me, "This is strings. This is a fucking spider web. God damnit, this is a whole damn rope."

"It's just flowers and chocolates, Eliza," he says, a defensive edge creeping into his tone. "It doesn't have to mean anything."

But it does. It means everything, and that's the problem.

"We can't do this," I say, hating the tremor in my voice. "We can't blur the lines like this. It's too complicated."

"What's complicated about it?" Chase challenges. "I care about you. You care about me. Why are we pretending otherwise?"

Because caring isn't enough. Because I'm your manager and you're my client. Because I have a son and responsibilities and a career I've worked my ass off for. Because I'm terrified of how much I feel for you.

I don't say any of that. Instead, I say, "You have a show tonight. You should be resting your voice, not... whatever this is."

Chase sighs, frustration evident. "Fine. Forget I did anything. I'll see you at soundcheck."

The line goes dead, and I'm left staring at the gifts on the bed. Part of me wants to throw them away, to erase this moment of weakness. But a larger part, the part I've been trying so hard to ignore, wants to cherish them.

I sink onto the bed, burying my face in my hands. This is exactly what I was afraid of. The lines are blurring, and I don't know how to stop it. Or if I even want to. What about the rules we set into place? What about *my* rule?

For a long time, I just sit there, letting the emotions wash over me. I think about Justin waiting for me back home. What would he think if he knew about this... arrangement I have with Chase? What kind of example am I setting?

Then there's my career to consider. I've worked too damn hard to get where I am. I've seen too many women in this industry sidelined because they got involved with artists. I swore I'd never be one of them. Not again. And yet here I am, teetering on the edge of exactly that.

But God, when I'm with Chase... it feels right. Like all the pieces of my life finally fit together. His laugh, his touch, the way he looks at me like I'm the only person in the world – it makes me feel alive in a way I haven't before in my life.

I stand up abruptly, pacing the room. This is insane. I'm acting like a lovesick teenager, not a grown woman with responsibilities. I need to end this, draw a clear line. It's the only way to protect myself, to protect the band, to protect Chase's career.

My eyes fall on the roses again, and I'm hit with a

memory. Chase, backstage after a show, his eyes shining with adrenaline and something else. The way he pulled me into a dark corner, his lips on mine, whispering "I need you" against my skin. The thrill, the danger, the overwhelming rightness of it all.

I shake my head, trying to clear the image. This is exactly why we can't do this. The intensity between us is too much. It'll consume everything if we let it.

With a deep breath, I reach for the roses, intending to throw them away. But as my fingers touch the soft petals, I hesitate. Maybe... maybe I can keep them. Just for today. A small indulgence before I do what needs to be done.

A knock at the door startles me out of my thoughts, and I instinctively throw the roses into a corner out of view. I open it to find Will, Incendiary Ink's drummer, looking uncomfortable.

"Hey, Eliza. Uh, have you seen Chase? He's not in his room, and we've got that radio interview in twenty."

I straighten, realizing how much time has passed while I drowned in my own selfish existential crisis, and slip back into manager mode, grateful for the distraction. "I'll find him. You guys go on ahead, we'll meet you there."

Will nods, then hesitates. "Everything okay? Chase seemed... off earlier."

"Everything's fine," I lie smoothly. "Just pre-show jitters. It's a big one tonight, right? I'll talk to him."

As soon as Will leaves, I grab my phone again, texting Chase.

ME: Where are you?

It takes a few minutes, but he finally replies.

CHASE: Hotel bar

Of course.

I find him nursing a whiskey, looking every inch the brooding rockstar. He doesn't look up as I slide onto the stool next to him.

"You have an interview in fifteen minutes," I say, keeping my voice neutral.

Chase takes another sip of his drink. "I know."

We sit in tense silence for a moment. Then, before I can stop myself, I say, "I'm sorry. About earlier. I... overreacted."

He finally looks at me, his green eyes intense. "Did you? Or were you just being honest for once?"

The question hangs between us, heavy with unsaid words we both know could destroy us. Destroy everything. Incendiary Ink on the brink of stardom, and I would only be a distraction for Chase. It would only complicate things and put everything we're working toward in jeopardy.

I open my mouth, then close it again, not sure how to respond. Because the truth is, I don't know. I don't know what I want, what I feel, what's right or wrong anymore. And if I can't say it, I shouldn't say anything. I can't muddy the water we're barely keeping our head's above or we'll all drown. Not just me. Not just Chase. Everyone.

Chase sighs, setting down his glass. "Look, Eliza. I know we said no strings. But I'm starting to think that's bullshit. There have always been strings between us. We're just too scared to admit it."

His words hit too close to home. Scared doesn't even begin to cover it. I can't give in to my emotions. I can't give in to *him.* It kills something inside of me to not openly agree with him, and I feel that death deep in my soul. I know exactly what I'm losing by not admitting my feelings right here and now, and my heart is pleading with me to just give in - but I just can't do it. Every path ahead that I see with us together ends in disaster for everyone involved. It's a responsibility I don't want. In fact, I want to run as far away from it as I fucking can.

But I can't.

We can't do this here. Hell, we can't do this anywhere. I pull myself together and stand abruptly. "We need to go. You can't be late for this interview."

Chase looks at me for a long moment, then nods, resignation settling over his features. "Sure. Whatever you say, boss."

As we walk to the elevator, I can feel the weight of everything unsaid between us. The roses and chocolates in my room. The ache in my chest. The knowledge that no matter how hard we try, 'no strings attached' might be an impossible dream for us.

The elevator doors close, and I catch our reflection in the mirrored walls. We're standing close, but not touching. Always close, but never quite connecting. I wonder how long we can keep this up before something breaks.

As we step out into the penthouse where the interview is being held, I push all these thoughts aside. Right now, I need to be Eliza Kerr, manager of Incendiary Ink. Not Eliza, the woman who's falling for her client despite her best efforts. Despite her own rules.

But as Chase's hand briefly brushes mine, sending a jolt of electricity through me, I know one thing for certain: This 'no strings' arrangement is far more complicated than either of us bargained for. And sooner or later, we're going to have to face the truth – whatever that might be.

Bad Guy

CHASE

THE VALET TAKES my keys with a nod of recognition. I wonder if he's an Incendiary Ink fan or if he just knows me as another washed-up rocker trying to relive his glory days. Either way, I force a smile and head into the restaurant, the scent of expensive perfume and seared meat hitting me as I enter.

La Boucle is exactly the kind of place Eliza would choose. Upscale without being pretentious, quiet enough for conversation but busy enough to provide a buffer of anonymity. As I follow the maître d', my heart pounds so loudly I'm sure everyone can hear it.

And then I see her.

Eliza is sitting at a corner table, her back to the wall – always aware of her surroundings, always in control. She's studying the menu, a strand of platinum blonde hair falling across her face. The sight of her hits me like a physical blow, and suddenly I'm transported back in time.

Eliza, laughing at something I said during a late-night recording session.

Eliza, fierce and protective, arguing with label execs on our behalf.

Eliza, her eyes filled with disappointment and pain the last time I saw her.

Guilt washes over me, so intense it makes me stumble. The maître d' gives me a concerned look, but I wave him off. I can't do this. I can't face her, can't confront the hurt I caused, the mess I made of everything.

I start to turn, ready to bolt, when Eliza looks up. Our eyes meet, and for a moment, the world stops spinning.

She's even more beautiful than I remembered. The years have been kind to her, adding a sophistication to her features that takes my breath away. But it's the vulnerability in her eyes, quickly masked, that roots me to the spot.

I've hurt her. God, I've hurt her so much. And yet here she is, willing to meet me, to give me another chance I don't deserve.

The least I can do is face her.

Taking a deep breath, I force myself to walk to the table. Eliza stands as I approach, and for an awkward moment, we both hesitate. Then, surprising us both, she steps forward and embraces me.

The hug is stiff, formal, nothing like the warm embraces we used to share. But feeling her in my arms again, smelling the familiar scent of her perfumes makes my head spin. It's never just one perfume. It's a mix of Chanel and something else. Something uniquely Eliza. I hold onto her a moment too long, savoring her scent and the contact I've been deprived of for five years.

Eliza pulls away first, a flicker of discomfort crossing her face. I immediately drop my arms, cursing myself for overstepping.

"Chase," she says, her voice steady but with an undercurrent I can't quite place. "You look well."

I manage a weak smile, trying to ignore the lingering warmth where her body pressed against mine. "Thanks. You look... amazing, Eliza. As always."

We sit, the tension between us palpable. I reach for the water glass, needing something to do with my hands. "Thanks for agreeing to meet me," I say, hating how formal I sound. "I know it can't be easy."

Eliza's expression softens slightly. "No, it's not. But it's necessary. We have a lot to discuss about the induction ceremony."

Right. The ceremony. The ostensible reason for this meeting. Not the years of history between us, not the unresolved feelings, not the apologies I owe her.

"Of course," I nod, reaching for the menu. "Should we order first?"

As we peruse the options, I steal glances at Eliza over the top of my menu. She's the picture of composure, but I can see the tension in the set of her shoulders, the way she grips the menu just a little too tightly. A memory flashes through my mind – Eliza, biting her lower lip in that same way as she read through our first record contract, determined to understand every clause.

I want to tell her how sorry I am. For everything. For the drugs, the erratic behavior, the cruel words I flung at her in the depths of my addiction. For not reaching out these past five years, for being too much of a coward to face what I'd done.

But the words stick in my throat. How do you apologize for destroying the best thing in your life? For hurting the person most important to you?

The waiter arrives to take our order, providing a momentary reprieve from the tension. As he walks away, Eliza fixes me with a look that used to mean she was about to lay down the law.

"Alright, Chase," she says, her tone all business. "Let's talk about the ceremony. The Hall of Fame has some specific requirements we need to go over."

I nod, grateful for the structure, the pretense of professionalism. But as Eliza starts outlining the details, I find myself studying her face, remembering all the times I've seen it: flushed with passion, creased with worry, soft with affection.

And I realize something that shakes me to my

core: I'm still in love with her. After all this time, after everything that's happened, I'm still hopelessly, irrevocably in love with Eliza Kerr.

The guilt threatens to overwhelm me again, but this time I push it down. I owe it to Eliza – and to myself – to be present for this conversation. To start making amends, even if it's just in small ways.

So, I lean in, forcing myself to focus on her words. "Okay," I say, meeting her gaze steadily for the first time. "Tell me what we need to do."

As Eliza continues talking, her voice washing over me like a familiar song, I make a silent promise to myself. I'm going to get through this dinner. I'm going to be professional and respectful. And somehow, someway, I'm going to find a way to make things right with the woman I never stopped loving.

It's the least I can do. For her, for us, for the memory of what we once were.

The waiter returns with our drinks, and as I raise my glass of sparkling water – a silent testament to my sobriety – I catch Eliza's eye. For a moment, just a fleeting second, I see a softness there, a hint of the connection we once shared.

It's not much. But it's enough to give me hope.

February 14, 2005 (Later that night)

The roar of the crowd still echoes in my ears as I stumble into my hotel room, a half-empty bottle of Jack in one hand and a giggling blonde in the other. I can't remember her name – Katie? Kristy? – but it doesn't matter. She's not the one I want to be with tonight.

"That was an amazing show," she purrs, pressing herself against me. Her perfume is too sweet, cloying, nothing like Eliza's sophisticated scent.

Eliza. The thought of her sends a fresh wave of anger and hurt through me. I take another swig from the bottle, welcoming the burn in my throat.

"You wanna know a secret?" I slur, pulling the blonde closer. "It's Valentine's Day, and the woman I lo— the woman I want doesn't want me."

She pouts, running a finger down my chest. "Aw, poor baby. I want you."

I laugh, a harsh, bitter sound. "Yeah? Then prove it."

I crash my lips against hers, the kiss sloppy and desperate. It's all wrong – her lips are too soft, her hair too straight, she tastes like strawberry lip gloss instead of Eliza's preferred mint – but I don't care. I just need to feel something, anything, other than this ache in my chest.

We stumble towards the bed, hands grasping, clothes being shed. I'm vaguely aware that this is a bad idea, that I'm making a mistake, but the alcohol and the hurt cloud my judgment.

Just as I'm about to push the blonde onto the bed, there's a knock at the door.

"Ignore it," I mutter, trailing kisses down her neck.

But then I hear it. Eliza's voice, muffled through the door but unmistakable.

"Chase? Are you in there? I... I wanted to talk about earlier."

Fuck.

I freeze, my blood turning to ice. For a moment, I consider not answering, pretending I'm not here. But I know Eliza. She won't give up that easily.

"Just a second!" I call out, my voice sounding strained even to my own ears.

I turn to the blonde – Kristy, I suddenly remember – who's looking confused and annoyed. "You need to hide," I hiss, gesturing towards the bathroom.

"Are you kidding me?" she huffs, but complies when she sees the panic in my eyes.

I scramble to pull on my jeans and t-shirt, running a hand through my disheveled hair in a futile attempt to look presentable. Taking a deep breath, I open the door.

Eliza stands there, looking breathtakingly beautiful and incredibly vulnerable. My heart clenches at the sight of her.

"Hey," I say, trying to sound casual and failing miserably. "What's up?"

Eliza's eyes narrow, taking in my disheveled appearance, the open bottle on the nightstand, the lingering scent of perfume in the air. I see the moment suspicion dawns in her eyes, but before she can say anything, a loud sneeze echoes from the bathroom.

Eliza's face falls, hurt and disappointment clouding her beautiful features. "I see you're busy," she says, her voice cold and laced with pain. "I'll talk to you in the morning."

"Eliza, wait—" I reach for her, but she steps back. This is all fucking wrong.

"Don't," she says, and the pain in her voice cuts through my drunken haze. "Just... don't, Chase. I can't believe I actually thought..." She trails off, shaking her head.

"It's not what you think," I plead, knowing how pathetic I sound.

"Really?" Eliza's laugh is bitter, and I can see her walls going back up – taller this time. "Because I think it's exactly what it looks like. You're drunk, and you've got some groupie hidden in your bathroom. The day you sent me flowers and tried to..." She stops, composing herself. "You know what? It doesn't matter. We're done here."

She turns and walks away, her heels clicking on the hotel's marble floor. I want to go after her, to explain, to beg for forgiveness, but I'm rooted to the spot. And I know any argument I give will be pointless and fall on deaf ears. I've just ruined any possibilities between us.

"Is she gone?" Kristy emerges from the bathroom, looking annoyed. "Can we get back to what we were doing?"

I look at her, feeling suddenly sober and incredibly tired. "You should go," I say quietly.

"Are you serious?" she scoffs. "You're choosing her? She doesn't even want you."

Her words hit too close to home. "Just fucking go," I repeat, more forcefully this time.

After Kristy leaves, slamming the door behind her, I sink to the floor, my back against the bed. I reach for the bottle of Jack, and take a long swig, trying to numb the pain etching its way jaggedly through my soul.

I pull out my phone, staring at Eliza's number. I should call her, try to explain. But what would I say? That I was hurt and drunk and stupid? That I didn't mean it? That I'm sorry?

Sorry doesn't begin to fucking cover it.

I throw the phone across the room in frustration, hearing it clatter against the wall. As I bury my face in my hands, the full weight of what just happened crashes down on me.

Eliza came to talk. She wanted to discuss things, maybe even change her mind about us. And I ruined it. I ruined everything.

The irony isn't lost on me. This morning, I sent her flowers and chocolates, wanting to show her how I felt. And now, not even twelve hours later, I've probably destroyed any chance we ever had.

Some Valentine's Day this turned out to be.

As I sit there in the dark, the taste of whiskey and regret bitter on my tongue, I wonder if Eliza will ever forgive me. If I'll ever forgive myself.

Somehow, I doubt it.

Anybody

ELIZA

THE WAITER CLEARS AWAY our plates, the clink of silverware against china punctuating the awkward silence that's fallen between us. Chase and I have exhausted all talk of the Hall of Fame ceremony, having dissected every detail from the seating arrangements to the setlist for the performance.

Now, with our professional obligations discussed, we're left with... what, exactly?

I take a sip of my wine, using the moment to study Chase over the rim of my glass. He looks good – sober suits him. The lines around his eyes speak of the years that have passed, but there's a clarity in his emerald gaze that I don't remember from before. It makes something twist in my chest, a mixture of pride and pain that I'm not ready to examine too closely.

"So," Chase says, breaking the silence and reading

my mind. As always. "I guess we've covered everything about the ceremony."

I nod, setting down my glass, trying desperately to keep my hand steady. "I think so. Unless you have any other questions?"

He shakes his head, and we lapse into silence again. I can feel the weight of unasked questions, of unspoken words, hanging heavy between us. There's so much I want to know, so much I need to understand if I'm going to get through the next few weeks of working with him.

But the pain of seeing him, of being reminded of everything we were and everything we lost, is still raw. It would be easier to call for the check, to walk away and keep things strictly professional.

Easier, but not better.

I take a deep breath, steeling myself. "Chase," I begin, my voice steadier than I feel, but still a little shaky. "I think we need to talk. About... everything."

He looks up, surprise and something like fear flickering in his eyes. "Yeah," he says softly. "I think we do."

I nod, gathering my courage. "Why didn't you respond when I reached out?" The question comes out before I can stop it, all the hurt and confusion of the past five years condensed into seven words.

Chase winces, guilt flashing across his face. "You tried to reach out?"

"Of course I did," I say, unable to keep the hurt

out of my voice. "For months after you got out of rehab. Calls, texts, emails. I even tried to contact you through your sponsor at the time. And Will and Mark. But you never replied. Not even through them. And what news I did get about you was vague and generic. It was like you'd disappeared. Like you didn't want me to even know you were okay."

He closes his eyes, pain etched across his features. "God, Eliza, I'm so sorry. I... I blocked your number. And the guys, and my sponsor... I made him promise not to pass on any messages."

"Why?" I ask, the old hurt bubbling up again, and now I can't seem to hide it. It's too powerful. "After everything we'd been through, why would you shut me out like that?"

Chase opens his eyes, and the raw anguish I see there takes my breath away. "Because I couldn't face you," he says, his voice barely above a whisper. "After the way I treated you at the end, the things I said, how I showed up that night... The guilt was too much. I thought... I thought you'd be better off without me in your life."

The memory of that night flashes through my mind – Chase, drunk and high, spewing venom and accusations, his words designed to cut deep. The pain of it, still fresh after all these years, makes me flinch.

"That wasn't your decision to make," I say, my voice tight with emotion. I said it on the phone before to him as well; he made that choice for me, effectively cutting me out completely.

"I know that now," Chase says, running a hand through his hair. "But back then, freshly sober, the guilt was overwhelming. And then... time just kept passing. Weeks turned into months, months into years. The longer I waited, the harder it became to reach out. I convinced myself it was too late, that you'd moved on and wouldn't want to hear from me anyway."

I take a deep breath, trying to steady myself. "I would have wanted to know you were okay," I say softly. "That you were staying sober, that you were healing. Do you have any idea what it was like, not knowing if you were even alive? There were months that even Will and Mark wouldn't get back to me."

Chase nods, understanding dawning in his eyes. "I never meant to hurt you like that. I was so caught up in my own guilt and shame that I couldn't see past it. I'm sorry, Eliza. I'm so fucking sorry."

His words hang in the air between us, heavy with regret and unspoken feelings. Part of me wants to accept his apology, to let go of the hurt I've been carrying for five years. But another part, the part that's been wounded too many times, holds back.

"I appreciate your apology, Chase," I say carefully. "But understanding why you did something doesn't automatically make it okay. You hurt me. Deeply. And that's not something I can just get over in one dinner conversation." And to be honest, even though he apologized, and I accept his words, I still don't fully understand it. I thought our connection back then was stronger than that. I don't know if I'll ever truly get over the hurt his shutting me out like that caused.

Chase nods, a mix of sadness and resignation in his eyes. "I understand. I don't expect forgiveness, Eliza. I just... I needed you to know how sorry I am."

I nod, acknowledging his words. "Are you... are you okay now?" I ask, changing the subject slightly.

A small smile tugs at the corner of Chase's mouth. "I'm sober," he says. "Five years, two months, and eleven days. It's not always easy, but... I'm doing okay."

Despite everything, I feel a surge of pride. "I'm glad," I say softly. "I always knew you could do it."

Something flashes in Chase's eyes at that – gratitude, maybe, or something deeper. "I couldn't have done it without you," he says. "Your support, even when I was at my worst... it meant everything, Eliza."

I feel tears pricking at the corners of my eyes and blink them back. This isn't how I expected this dinner to go, but I realize that this is what I needed – not closure, exactly, but a start. A chance to see the man Chase has become, to begin to reconcile him with the man I knew.

"Where do we go from here?" I ask, the question

encompassing so much more than just the upcoming ceremony.

Chase looks at me for a long moment, his gaze intense. "I don't know," he admits. "But I'd like to find out. If you're willing."

I take a deep breath, weighing his words. There's still so much unsaid between us, so much to work through. And despite the feelings I know I still have for him, I can't ignore the years of pain and the breach of trust.

"I think," I say slowly, "that we need to take this one step at a time. We have a couple of months of working together ahead of us with this Hall of Fame induction. Let's see how that goes first."

Chase nods, a mix of hope and understanding in his eyes. "That sounds fair. I know I have a lot to prove, Eliza. And I'm willing to do whatever it takes."

"It's not about proving anything, Chase," I say, surprising myself with my candor. "It's about rebuilding trust. And that takes time."

"Time," he repeats softly. "Yeah, I can do that."

As we call for the check, I feel a strange mix of emotions. There's still hurt, still anger at what happened between us. But there's also a glimmer of something else. Not forgiveness, not yet. But maybe... possibility.

We step out into the cool night air, and for a moment, we just stand there, neither quite ready to say goodbye.

"Thank you," Chase says finally. "For giving me a chance to explain. For... for everything, really."

I nod, offering a small smile. "Thank you for being honest. It's a start."

The valet approaches with my car keys, and I feel a sudden reluctance to leave. Chase seems to sense it, shifting his weight from one foot to the other.

"So, I guess this is goodnight," he says, his voice soft.

"I guess it is," I reply, equally quiet.

We stand there for another moment, the air between us charged with lingering emotions. Finally, I take a deep breath and turn to the valet.

"Thank you," I say, accepting my keys.

As I settle into my car, I watch Chase in the rearview mirror as he waits for his own vehicle. He looks lost in thought, his brow furrowed in that way I remember so well.

I start the engine, but before I pull away, I allow myself one last look at him. Our eyes meet briefly, and he offers a small, tentative wave. I return it, feeling a mix of emotions I can't quite name.

As I drive away, I realize that this dinner hasn't given me the closure I thought I wanted. Instead, it's opened a door I thought was long closed. And while I'm not ready to step through it just yet, I find myself, for the first time in five years, not wanting to slam it shut either.

The next couple of months are going to be interesting, to say the least. But as I navigate the familiar streets of Los Angeles, I realize I'm looking forward to seeing what happens next. And that, in itself, feels like progress.

September 15, 2006

The diamond on my left hand catches the morning sunlight as I reach for my latte, sending little prisms dancing across the coffee shop wall. I still can't quite believe it's there – three weeks engaged, and it still feels surreal.

I glance at my watch. Twenty minutes until the first Incendiary Ink band meeting since their break began six months ago. Plenty of time to savor my coffee and gather my thoughts. It's been a whirlwind half-year – the band's break, throwing myself into other projects at Blackmore, and then meeting Clive.

Clive. My fiancé. Successful music promoter, charming, stable. Everything I should want. Everything I do want. Right? The speed of our relationship sometimes makes my head spin, but isn't that what love is supposed to do?

The bell over the door chimes, and I look up out of habit. My heart stops.

Chase.

He's let his hair grow out again, and there's a scruffy beard shadowing his jaw. But those green eyes are the same, lighting up with recognition as they land on me. For a moment, I forget how to breathe.

"Well, well, well," he drawls, a slow smile spreading across his face as he approaches my table. "If it isn't the elusive Eliza Kerr. I was starting to think you were just a figment of my imagination."

I stand, a mix of emotions swirling in my chest. It's been six months since we've seen each other, not since that disastrous night after their last show. "Chase. Hi. It's... it's good to see you."

He nods, his eyes roaming my face as if relearning it. "You too. You look great. Time off from babysitting us clearly agrees with you."

I can't help but laugh. "Funny, I was just thinking how relaxed you look. The break seems to be working wonders."

Chase shrugs, that familiar half-smile tugging at his lips. "Well, you know what they say. Absence makes the heart grow fonder and the liver recover."

"Chase," I admonish, but there's no heat in it. I've missed this easy banter between us.

His eyes drop to my hand, and I see the exact moment he notices the diamond. His expression flickers – surprise, then something that looks almost like pain before he schools his features into a teasing grin.

"Wow," he says, his voice light but with an undercurrent I can't quite place. "That's some rock. Did you find a sugar daddy while we were away, or did you rob a jewelry store?"

I roll my eyes, fighting the urge to hide my hand. "Very funny. His name is Clive. Clive Baxter. He's a music promoter. We met at the Summer Sonic Festival in Tokyo."

Recognition flashes in Chase's eyes. "Clive Baxter? Tall guy, always wears those ugly paisley ties?"

I nod, surprised, purposely ignoring the tie comment. "You know him?"

Chase's grin turns a bit forced and my heart lurches. "Yeah, we've crossed paths a few times. Small world, huh? Well, congrats, Eliza. I'm happy for you. Really."

There's an awkward pause, filled with all the things we're not saying. I find myself searching his face, trying to read what he's really thinking. Is he upset? Jealous? Or am I just projecting, wanting to see something that isn't there?

"So," Chase says, breaking the silence. "Six months, huh? Feels like a lifetime. The guys are pretty excited about getting back in the studio. Think you can still handle us, or has your new romance made you soft?"

I arch an eyebrow at him. "Please. I could manage you boys in my sleep. In fact, I'm pretty sure I have."

Chase laughs, a genuine sound that makes something in my chest ache. "There's the Eliza we know and fear. God, I've missed this. Missed you."

The words hit me like a physical blow. I look up at him, and for a moment, I see everything we used to be, everything we could have been. And suddenly, I'm not sure of anything anymore.

"I've missed you too," I admit softly, the words slipping out before I can stop them.

We stand there for a moment, the air between us charged with unspoken feelings and missed opportunities. Then Chase clears his throat, breaking the spell.

"We should probably head over," he says, gesturing towards the door. "Don't want to be late for our own resurrection, right?"

I nod, gathering my things. As we walk towards the Blackmore offices, I'm acutely aware of the space between us – close enough to touch, but separated by choices and circumstances and the glittering diamond on my finger.

I think about Clive, probably already at work, planning his next big event. Steady, reliable Clive, who swept me off my feet in a whirlwind romance. Then I look at Chase, wild and unpredictable and so achingly familiar, and I feel my carefully constructed world start to tilt on its axis.

What am I doing? Is Clive just another project, something to distract me from the complicated mess of feelings I have for Chase?

As we step into the elevator, I catch our reflection in the mirrored walls, something I'm so used to doing with us. Chase and Eliza, together again. It looks right in a way I'm not prepared to examine too closely.

"So," Chase says as the doors close, his tone deceptively casual. "You and Clive, huh? Must be pretty serious if there's a ring involved."

I nod, twisting the diamond absently. "It is. It's... fast, but when you know, you know. Right?"

Chase's smile doesn't quite reach his eyes. "Right. Of course."

The elevator starts to move, and I take a deep breath. Two months until the wedding – a fact I'm grateful I haven't shared with Chase. Two months to figure out if I'm making the biggest mistake of my life, or finally doing something right.

God help me.

Pieces

CHASE

THE LOS ANGELES traffic crawls along the 101, but for once, I don't mind. The slow pace gives me time to process Dr. Hendricks' words from our therapy session.

"Seeing Eliza again has stirred up a lot of old feelings, Chase. That's natural. The question is, what are you going to do with those feelings?"

I drum my fingers on the steering wheel, the rhythm matching the tumult in my head. What am I going to do? Hell if I know.

Five years of sobriety, of working on myself, of trying to become someone I could be proud of. And one dinner with Eliza has me feeling like that lost, confused kid all over again.

I've always preferred these one-on-one sessions with Dr. Hendricks. AA meetings in LA are about as anonymous as a billboard on Sunset Boulevard. But today, part of me wishes for the simplicity of those meetings. "Hi, I'm Chase, and I'm an alcoholic" is a hell of a lot easier than "Hi, I'm Chase, and I'm still in love with the woman I hurt beyond measure five years ago."

My phone buzzes with a text from Will.

> WILL: You close? Mark's already here, threatening to start without us.

I smile despite myself. Some things never change.

Twenty minutes later, I'm pulling into the driveway of Will's Malibu home. It's been a few months since we've all been together like this. Sure, we've seen each other over the past five years - birthdays, holidays, the occasional jam session. But this feels different. This feels like it matters.

Mark's cherry-red vintage Mustang is already in the driveway, parked next to Will's sleek Tesla. The contrast makes me chuckle. We may be older, but some dynamics remain the same.

I find them in Will's home studio, Mark already coaxing a melody from his Gibson, while Will absently taps a rhythm on his thighs. Even after all these years, they're both unfairly handsome. Will's dark hair is artfully tousled, not a trace of gray despite being in our forties. Mark, ever the rebel, still sports a shock of electric blue running through his otherwise golden locks.

"Look what the cat dragged in," Will grins,

unfolding his tall frame from behind his drum kit to pull me into a quick hug. His arms, still muscled from years of drumming, nearly squeeze the breath out of me.

"How ya been, man?" Mark asks, setting his guitar aside. He's kept himself fit too, his lean physique a testament to clean living and probably way too much yoga.

"Can't complain," I shrug, clapping them both on the shoulder. It's surreal sometimes, how we've all grown up but somehow stayed the same. "How about you guys?"

Mark fixes me with a knowing look. "Better than you, I'd guess. Heard you had dinner with Eliza."

I freeze, caught off guard. "How did you-"

"Dude," Will laughs, running a hand through his thick hair, "it's us. Did you really think we wouldn't know?"

I sigh, sinking into the worn leather couch. "It was... intense. Good, I think. But complicated."

They exchange a look I can't quite decipher. "You okay?" Will asks, his tone softer.

I nod, not quite meeting their eyes. "Yeah, I'm good. It's just... a lot, you know?"

Mark nods sagely, idly strumming a chord. "We know, man. We were there for most of it, remember?"

The weight of our shared history hangs in the air for a moment before Will claps his hands, breaking the tension.

"Alright, enough of this sappy shit. We've got work to do. Hall of Fame, boys! Can you believe it?"

I can't help but grin. His excitement is infectious. "Still feels fucking surreal," I admit, my fingers instinctively moving to form bass chords even without my instrument.

"Well, believe it," Mark says, tossing his blue-streaked hair out of his eyes. "Now we just need to decide what to play. We get three songs, right?"

I nod, grateful for the change of subject. "Yeah, three songs to sum up our entire career. No pressure or anything."

Will grabs his drumsticks, tapping absently. "Well, we gotta do *Off the Record,* right? It was our first big hit."

"Agreed," Mark nods. "And *Burning Bridges* has to be in there. It was huge, and it kinda defined our sound for our third album."

I swallow hard, memories flooding back. That song, written when I was teetering on the edge, pouring all my pain and confusion into the lyrics. Eliza's face when she first heard it, worry and sadness warring in her eyes.

"Yeah," I say, my voice rougher than I intend. "Yeah, let's do *Burning Bridges.*"

Will eyes me carefully. "You sure, man? We can pick something else if it's too much."

I shake my head. "No, it's perfect. It's... it's part of our story, you know? The good and the bad."

They both nod, understanding.

"Okay," Mark says, "so we've got *Off the Record* and *Burning Bridges*. What about the last one?"

I think for a moment, then a slow smile spreads across my face. "What about *Whispered Truths*?"

Will's eyes widen, a knowing look passing between him and Mark. "Seriously? You want to do that one?"

I nod, my heart racing a little. "Yeah, I do. It was a big hit, and the fans love it. Plus..." I trail off, not sure how to put it into words.

"Plus, it's about Eliza," Mark finishes softly.

I nod again, not trusting my voice. *Whispered Truths* had been our closing song for years, a power ballad that always brought the house down. What the fans didn't know was that I'd written it for Eliza, pouring all my complicated feelings for her into every line. Fuck, in truth – *every* song was for her in some way.

"You think she knows?" Will asks, his voice gentle.

I shrug, trying for nonchalance and probably failing miserably. "I don't know. Maybe. We never really talked about it."

There's a moment of silence as we all remember those days - the tension, the unspoken feelings, the way Eliza would watch from the wings every time we performed that song, her expression unreadable.

"I think it's perfect," Mark says finally. "It showcases a different side of our sound, and it was a fan favorite. Plus..." he grins, lightening the mood, "it'll give the ladies in the audience something to swoon over."

I roll my eyes, but I'm grateful for the break in tension. "Alright, alright. So we're agreed? *Off the Record, Burning Bridges,* and *Whispered Truths*?"

Will and Mark nod, and just like that, it's decided.

"Well then," Mark says, strumming the opening chords of *Whispered Truths,* "shall we run through them? For old times' sake?"

As we start to play, the familiar melodies washing over me, I feel something stir in my chest. This - the music, the brotherhood - this has always been my constant. Through the highs and lows, the addiction and recovery, the love and loss, the music has always been there.

And as we launch into *Whispered Truths,* I can't help but think of Eliza. I wonder if she'll understand the significance when we play it at the ceremony. If she'll remember all those nights, all those unspoken words between us.

"You know," Will says during a break, "we should probably run this set list by Eliza. Make sure she's cool with it for the induction speech and all."

I nod, trying to ignore the way my heart races at the thought of discussing this particular song choice with Eliza. "Yeah, you're right. I'll give her a call tomorrow."

As we dive back into the music, I can't help but feel like we're not just rehearsing for a performance. We're opening a door to something new, something that bridges our past and our future.

I guess I'll find out soon enough where that door leads.

Run

ELIZA

THE STEADY CLICK of my Louboutin boots echoes through the halls of Blackmore Records, a rhythm as familiar as any hit single we've produced. It's barely 8 AM, but my mind is already a cacophony of tasks: Hall of Fame logistics, contract negotiations for Lila Rose (our newest indie-pop sensation), and the never-ending battle with my inbox.

And underneath it all, a persistent bassline of thoughts about Chase and our dinner.

I'm so engrossed in mental calculations about Lila's streaming projections that I nearly collide with Michelle as I round the corner.

"Woah there, boss lady," she laughs, steadying me with a hand on my arm. "You know, if you keep avoiding me, I might start to take it personally."

I wince, guilt flashing through me. I have been

avoiding her, haven't I? "Sorry, Michelle. I've just been..."

"Busy?" she finishes, raising an eyebrow. "Too busy to tell your best friend how that dinner went? The dinner you've been stressing about for days?"

I sigh, ushering her into my office and closing the door. The familiar scent of her jasmine perfume follows us in, a reminder of countless late-night strategy sessions and confidential chats. "It's not that I didn't want to tell you. It's just..."

"Complicated?" Michelle supplies, perching on the edge of my desk.

I nod, sinking into my chair. "How'd you guess?"

She rolls her eyes good-naturedly. "Please. It's you and Chase. When has it ever not been complicated?"

I turn to my dual monitors, pulling up Lila's projected numbers as a distraction. "It was... good. Professional. He looks healthy. Five years sober."

"But?" Michelle prompts, undeterred.

I pause, my cursor hovering over a particularly promising streaming forecast. "But... it's like no time has passed and all the time in the world has passed, all at once. He's still Chase, you know? Still has that way of looking at me like..."

"Like you're the only person in the room?" Michelle finishes softly.

I nod, not trusting my voice.

"And that scares you."

"Wouldn't it scare you?" I ask, finally looking up at her. "After everything that happened? The rehab, the things he said, the years of silence?"

Michelle considers this, absently fiddling with a golden record on my wall - Incendiary Ink's second album. "Yeah, it would. But Eliza, at some point you have to decide if the potential for happiness outweighs the fear of getting hurt again. You can't keep producing other people's love songs if you're not willing to star in your own."

Before I can respond, my phone buzzes. It's a text from Chase.

> CHASE: Band rehearsal at 2. Song choices finalized. You should be there.

I show the text to Michelle, who raises an eyebrow. "Well, looks like the universe is giving you a push. You going?"

I hesitate, my mind already conjuring up a list of excuses. Board meetings. Conference calls. Lila's contract. But I know none of them will stick. "I have to. It's my job, after all."

Michelle stands, heading for the door. "Sure, keep telling yourself that's the only reason. Just... keep an open mind, okay?"

As she leaves, I turn back to my computer, trying to lose myself in contract negotiations and damage control. But my mind keeps drifting to the upcoming rehearsal, to seeing Chase again, to hearing the songs they've chosen.

Before I know it, it's 1:45 and I'm pulling into the parking lot of Sonic Boom Studios. The faded mural of music legends on the exterior wall brings back a flood of memories - late night recording sessions, heated creative debates, stolen moments in dark corners.

I take a deep breath, the familiar scent of old cigarette smoke and stale coffee hitting me as I enter. Some things never change.

The sound of music greets me as I step into Studio A. They're in the middle of *Off the Record*, and for a moment, I'm transported back in time. Chase's voice, still as powerful and emotive as ever, wraps around me like a familiar embrace. The years fall away, and I'm that young A&R rep again, watching her first big signing take flight.

Will sees me first, offering a wave from behind his drum kit, never missing a beat. Mark nods in acknowledgment, fingers flying across his guitar strings in that intricate bridge section that always impressed me. And Chase... Chase's eyes lock with mine, a small smile playing at his lips as he continues to sing, his fingers never faltering on his bass.

They finish the song, and after a brief discussion filled with the shorthand of a band that's been together for decades, they launch into *Burning Bridges*. It's a harder song, full of pain and anger, and

I remember all too well the tumultuous time when it was written. I see Chase's jaw clench on certain lines, and I wonder if he's remembering too.

But it's the third song that changes everything.

The opening chords of *Whispered Truths* fill the room, and I feel my breath catch. I've always loved this song, but something feels different this time. Maybe it's the way Chase's voice softens on certain lines, or the way his eyes keep finding mine as he sings, as if each word is meant for me alone.

And suddenly, like feedback from an amp turned up too high, it hits me. The lyrics I've heard a hundred times before suddenly take on new meaning:

In the silence between words,
In the spaces we don't fill,
There's a truth we've never heard,
A promise we can't fulfill.

It's about me. About us. All this time, and I never realized.

I watch Chase as he sings, really watch him, and I see every emotion play across his face. The love, the regret, the hope - it's all there, laid bare in the lyrics and the melody.

As the last notes fade away, I find myself blinking back tears, grateful for the dim lighting of the studio. Chase is looking at me, a question in his eyes, and I know he's wondering if I've finally understood.

The realization that this song - this beautiful, heart-wrenching song - is about me sends a rush of warmth through my body. For a moment, I allow myself to bask in it, to imagine what it might be like to let those walls down and let Chase in again.

But then reality comes crashing back. The years of pain, the broken trust, the professional complications - they all flood my mind, dousing the warm glow of realization with cold, hard facts.

Yes, the song is about me. Yes, Chase clearly had - maybe still has - deep feelings for me. But is that enough? Can it overcome all the hurt, all the challenges we'd face?

As the band starts to pack up their gear, I find myself rooted to the spot, my mind a whirlwind of conflicting emotions. Chase hands his bass to a tech and approaches, that familiar half-smile on his face.

"So, what did you think?" he asks, his voice soft, intimate.

I swallow hard, forcing a professional smile. "It was great. You guys are going to bring the house down at the ceremony."

Something flickers in Chase's eyes - disappointment? Resignation? - but he nods, keeping his tone light. "That's the plan. Thanks for coming, Eliza. It means a lot."

He pauses, running a hand through his hair - a gesture so familiar it makes my heart ache. "Listen, I was wondering if maybe we could grab a coffee or something? Talk about the set list, make sure we're on the same page for the ceremony."

I hesitate, every instinct screaming at me to make an excuse, to maintain that professional distance. But the hopeful look in his eyes weakens my resolve. "I don't know, Chase. We covered most of the details at dinner..."

"I know," he says quickly. "I just thought... well, it's been a while since we really talked. About everything."

The implied meaning hangs heavy between us. *Everything*. Our past, our missed chances, the constant bad timing that's defined our relationship.

"Chase," I start, my voice barely above a whisper, "I'm not sure that's a good idea."

He takes a step closer, and I catch a whiff of his cologne - the same one he's worn for years. It brings back a flood of memories: stolen moments during recording sessions, the bittersweet realization during my second marriage that I was still in love with him, the gut-wrenching news of his Vegas wedding just as I was finalizing my divorce.

"Why not?" he asks softly. "We're both adults, Eliza. We can handle a conversation, can't we?"

I look up at him, *really* look at him. The years have been kind to Chase, adding a maturity to his features that only enhances his appeal. But it's the vulnerability in his eyes that catches me off guard.

"It's complicated," I say, echoing my earlier words

to Michelle. "There's a lot of history there. A lot of... missed timing."

Chase nods, a sad smile playing at his lips. "I know. That's kind of why I want to talk. Clear the air, maybe? Start fresh?"

For a moment, I'm tempted. The idea of starting fresh, of wiping the slate clean and seeing where things might go... it's intoxicating. But then I remember all the times I've made the wrong choice, all the heartache that's followed.

"I appreciate the offer, Chase," I say finally, straightening my shoulders. "But I think it's best if we keep things professional. For now, at least."

The disappointment is clear on his face, but he nods, respecting my decision. "I understand. But Eliza?"

"Yes?"

"The offer stands. If you ever change your mind... well, you know where to find me. And for what it's worth, I'm sorry. For everything. The timing, the mistakes... all of it."

As I turn to leave, Chase calls out one last time. "Oh, and Eliza? *Whispered Truths*... it was always about you. I thought you should know that."

The words hit me like a physical blow, confirming what I'd just realized. I manage a nod, not trusting myself to speak, and hurry out of the studio.

As I step into the warm Los Angeles afternoon, the echo of *Whispered Truths* still ringing in my ears,

I'm not sure which way the scales will tip. The professional in me knows I made the right call. But the woman who's carried a torch for Chase all these years, through failed marriages and missed opportunities? She's screaming at me to turn around, to take that chance.

For the first time in a long time, I'm willing to consider the possibility that maybe, just maybe, some risks are worth taking. But am I brave enough to break the cycle of bad timing and wrong choices? Can I trust myself to make the right decision this time?

Only time will tell. But as I drive away from the studio, Chase's words echoing in my mind, I can't help but wonder: what if this time, finally, our timing is right?

March 13, 2008

The scratch of pen on paper seems unnaturally loud in the sterile conference room. I sign my name with a flourish - Eliza Kerr, not Baxter - officially ending my second marriage after just over a year.

"Congratulations, Ms. Kerr," my lawyer says, her voice tinged with the awkward cheer of someone who's not sure if congratulations are appropriate. "You're officially divorced."

I nod, not trusting my voice. Relief mingles with a profound sense of failure as I gather my things. Another marriage, another mistake. As I step out into the bright Los Angeles sunshine, I can't help but wonder: why do I keep making the wrong choices?

Little do I know, at that very moment, 270 miles away in Las Vegas, Chase Avery is making a choice of his own - one that will send shockwaves through both our lives.

Days pass in a blur of work and carefully constructed avoidance of anything personal. I throw myself into contracts, marketing plans, anything to keep my mind off the empty house I return to each night.

It's nearly a week later when I finally allow myself a moment to breathe. I'm curled up on my couch, a glass of wine in hand, mindlessly flipping through a stack of industry magazines when a headline catches my eye, and my world tilts on its axis:

"INCENDIARY INK FRONTMAN CHASE AVERY'S SURPRISE VEGAS WEDDING!"

The wine glass slips from my suddenly numb fingers, spilling red across my white carpet. I barely notice. My eyes are glued to the page, drinking in the grainy paparazzi shot of Chase stumbling out of a chapel, a blonde in a mini dress clinging to his arm.

The article is a blur of sensationalized details - a

whirlwind romance, a drunken ceremony, speculation about the band's future. But all I can focus on is the date: March 13th. The exact same day my divorce was finalized. While I was signing away one failed marriage, Chase was stumbling into his own.

A laugh bubbles up in my throat, bitter and bordering on hysterical. Of course. Of course this would happen on the same day. Our timing has always been spectacularly, cosmically bad.

Unbidden, a memory surfaces: Chase and I, late night in the studio, just a month ago. The band was on a break, and I was already knee-deep in divorce proceedings that I'd kept to myself. Chase was playing a new song, something raw and beautiful that never made it onto an album.

"What do you think?" he'd asked, his eyes seeking mine in that way that always made my heart skip.

"It's beautiful," I'd said, meaning it. "But sad."

He'd shrugged, a half-smile playing on his lips. "Sometimes the best songs come from the saddest places."

I'd felt it then, the pull between us that had always been there. For a moment, I'd let myself imagine what it would be like to give in, to let myself fall. But then my wedding ring had caught the light, and I'd remembered why I couldn't. *Not yet.* Soon, maybe – if I was brave enough.

Now, staring at the news of Chase's impulsive marriage, performed at the exact moment I was freeing myself from my own, I wonder if that moment had meant as much to him as it had to me. Or if, perhaps, it had scared him into this rash decision.

The next few weeks are a whirlwind of rumors and speculation. The industry gossip mill is working overtime, and despite my best efforts to stay professional, bits and pieces reach my ears. Chase's new wife is a cocktail waitress he met the night of the wedding. He was on a bender when it happened. He's already talking to lawyers about an annulment.

Each new piece of information is a knife to my heart. I try to tell myself it's just concern for the band, for the brand we've built. But in the quiet moments, I can't deny the truth: it hurts because it's Chase.

Before I know it, it's time for the band's reunion meeting. As I step into the conference room at Blackmore Records, the tension is palpable. Will and Mark are already there, greeting me with awkward smiles. And then Chase walks in.

He looks... rough. Like he hasn't slept in weeks. But still, damn him, unfairly handsome. Our eyes meet, and for a moment, it's like no time has passed at all.

"Eliza," he says, his voice soft, almost reverent. "It's good to see you."

"You too," I manage, proud of how steady my voice sounds. "Congratulations on your marriage."

Pain flashes across his face, quickly replaced by

shame. "Thanks," he says, the word sounding forced. "I heard about your divorce. I'm sorry."

The meeting passes in a haze of contract discussions and tour planning. I'm hyperaware of Chase's presence, of every move he makes, every word he speaks. The chemistry between us, that spark that's always been there, feels stronger than ever.

As the meeting wraps up, I head to the kitchenette for a much-needed coffee. I'm reaching for the pot when a familiar presence appears beside me.

"Still mainlining caffeine, I see," Chase says, a hint of his old teasing tone in his voice.

I turn, and suddenly we're too close. I can smell his cologne, see the flecks of gold in his green eyes. "Some things never change," I say, aiming for lightness but hearing the tremor in my voice.

"And some things do," he murmurs, his eyes searching mine. "Eliza, I... I made a mistake. A huge mistake."

My heart races. Is he talking about the wedding? About us? Before I can ask, he continues.

"I'm talking to lawyers. About an annulment. It... it never should have happened."

For a moment, I let myself imagine closing the distance between us, consequences be damned. The air feels charged, electric. Chase leans in, just slightly, and I find myself swaying towards him.

"Hey, Chase! We need you to sign off on these tour dates!"

Mark's voice shatters the moment. Chase steps back, clearing his throat. "I should go," he says, regret clear in his voice. "But Eliza... can we talk? Later? There's so much I need to say."

I nod, not trusting myself to speak. As he walks away, I let out a shaky breath. What just happened?

Later, alone in my office, I try to make sense of it all. The divorce, Chase's marriage and impending annulment, the undeniable pull between us that still exists. I know I need to be professional, to keep things strictly business. But a small, traitorous part of me whispers: what if this is our chance?

As I start drafting an email about the upcoming tour, I make a decision. I'll keep things professional, for now. I'll be the manager they need me to be. But I'll also listen to what Chase has to say. Because if there's one thing I've learned, it's that when it comes to Chase Avery, my heart can't be trusted to make the right choice.

But maybe, just maybe, this time it's not about making the right choice. Maybe it's about taking a risk on the only choice that's ever felt truly right.

Chains (The Tower)

CHASE

THE LEATHER COUCH creaks as I shift uncomfortably, my fingers drumming an erratic beat on my knee. Dr. Hendricks watches me with that patient, knowing look I've come to both appreciate and dread over the past five years.

"So, Chase," he begins, his voice calm and steady, "how did the rehearsal go?"

I shrug, aiming for nonchalance and probably missing by a mile. "Fine. Good. The guys are in top form. We're gonna kill it at the ceremony."

Dr. Hendricks nods, but I can tell he's not buying my act. "And Eliza? How was it seeing her again?"

The question hits me like a sucker punch, even though I knew it was coming. I've been dreading it since I walked in here.

"It was... fine," I manage, wincing at how unconvincing I sound.

"Chase," Dr. Hendricks says gently, "we've talked about this. Honesty, remember? Even when it's difficult. Especially when it's difficult."

I sigh, running a hand through my hair. "Okay, fine. It was... intense. Seeing her there, hearing us play *Whispered Truths*... It brought up a lot of stuff."

"What kind of stuff?"

I close my eyes, remembering the way Eliza looked as we played. The emotions that flickered across her face, the way her eyes never left mine during the chorus.

"Everything," I admit quietly. "All the feelings I thought I'd dealt with. All the regrets, the what-ifs. It's like... it's like no time has passed at all."

Dr. Hendricks leans forward slightly. "Chase, have you considered that perhaps these feelings were never truly dormant?"

The question catches me off guard, but as I think about it, I realize he's right. "I guess... I guess they've always been there, just under the surface. I've just gotten good at ignoring them."

"And now?"

"Now?" I laugh, but there's no humor in it. "Now I don't know if I can ignore them anymore. But I'm scared, doc. What if... what if feeling this way puts my sobriety at risk?"

Dr. Hendricks considers this for a moment. "Chase, recovery isn't about not feeling. It's about learning to feel without turning to destructive behaviors. But let's talk about why these feelings scare you so much."

I swallow hard, knowing where this is going. "Because of what I did. How I hurt her."

"Can you tell me about that? About the last time you saw Eliza before rehab?"

My chest tightens at the thought. "Do we have to go there?"

"I think we do," Dr. Hendricks says gently. "Sometimes we need to confront our past to move forward."

I take a deep breath, forcing myself back to that day. The memories come flooding back, vivid and painful.

"I was... I was a mess. Coming off a three-day bender. I showed up at her place, ranting about some perceived slight. God, I don't even remember what I was angry about. But I remember the look on her face. Disappointment. Sadness. Fear."

I pause, the shame of that day washing over me anew.

"I said... horrible things. Accused her of holding me back, of trying to control me. I told her she was the reason the band was falling apart. That she... that she meant nothing to me."

My voice breaks on the last words. Dr. Hendricks hands me a tissue, and I realize I'm crying.

"The worst part," I continue, "is that she just stood there and took it. She'd always been there for me, through everything. And that's how I repaid her."

"Thank you for sharing that, Chase," Dr. Hendricks says after a moment. "That couldn't have been easy. Now, looking back, what do you think about your actions that day?"

I laugh bitterly. "I think I was a selfish, destructive asshole who hurt the one person who always had my back."

Dr. Hendricks nods. "And have you ever apologized to Eliza for this specific incident?"

The question makes me shift uncomfortably, the leather couch squeaking beneath me. I can feel a bead of sweat forming on my brow. "I've apologized to her in general terms. You know, for everything that happened, for how I acted during that time. But for that specific day? No, I... I haven't."

"Why do you think that is, Chase?"

I let out a long breath, my gaze drifting to the abstract painting on the wall, its swirls of blue and gray suddenly fascinating. "I guess... I've been afraid to bring it up. To remind her of how awful I was. And maybe... maybe I've been afraid to really face it myself."

Dr. Hendricks leans forward, his elbows on his knees. "Chase, there's a difference between a general apology and taking specific accountability for our actions. Why do you think it might be important to address specific incidents?"

The question hangs in the air, heavy with responsibility I'm not sure I want to take on. I can feel my heart rate picking up. "Because... because it shows I remember. That I understand the real impact of what I did, not just in some vague, general sense."

"Exactly," Dr. Hendricks nods approvingly. "And what do you think it might mean to Eliza to hear you acknowledge specific moments?"

I close my eyes, imagining Eliza's face, the hurt I've seen there too many times. "It would show her that I really understand what I put her through. That I'm not just sorry in some abstract way, but that I get how my actions affected her."

"That's very insightful, Chase. Now, let's talk about accountability. How is that different from just apologizing?"

I run a hand through my hair, thinking. "Accountability is... it's owning what I did. Not making excuses or blaming it on the drugs or alcohol. It's saying 'I did this, and I understand how it hurt you.'"

"And why have you avoided this level of accountability until now?"

The question hits me like a punch to the gut. I can feel my throat tightening. "Because I'm ashamed," I admit, my voice barely above a whisper. "Because facing the specifics of what I did, really looking at it... it's painful. And I guess I've been a coward about it."

Dr. Hendricks' expression softens. "It takes

courage to admit that, Chase. Now, the question is, what are you going to do about it?"

I take a deep breath, feeling a mix of fear and determination. "I need to talk to her. *Really* talk to her. About that day, about everything. No more hiding behind general apologies or vague acknowledgments."

"That sounds like a good plan. But before you do that, I want you to do something. Write a letter to Eliza. Don't send it, just write it. Be specific. Address the incidents you've avoided talking about. Express your regret, your understanding of how your actions affected her, and your commitment to genuine accountability. Can you do that?"

I nod, feeling a strange mix of dread and relief. "Yeah. Yeah, I can do that."

As I leave the office and slide into my car, I sit for a moment, letting out a long breath. The idea of confronting my past mistakes in such specific detail, of laying bare my regrets to Eliza, terrifies me. But for the first time in a long time, I feel like I'm on the right path.

I start the engine, my mind already composing the opening lines of a letter that will force me to face the worst parts of my past. It won't be easy, but maybe, just maybe, this will be the first step towards truly making things right with Eliza.

September 15, 2010

The neon lights of the Las Vegas strip paint my hotel room in an eerie glow, a kaleidoscope of colors that does nothing to settle my nerves. I pace back and forth, my bare feet sinking into the plush carpet with each step. The bass from the casino below thrums through the floor, a constant reminder of the show we just finished and the one looming tomorrow.

My eyes keep darting to the mini-bar. The little bottles glint in the low light, promising a temporary respite from the chaos in my head. I shouldn't. I know I shouldn't. But God, I want to.

Vegas. It had to be fucking Vegas. Every street, every gaudy casino is a reminder of that night two years ago. The night I made the stupidest decision of my life, stumbling drunk into a chapel with a woman whose name I could barely remember. The marriage lasted all of three months, but the guilt... that's stuck around a lot longer.

A knock at the door breaks through my spiraling thoughts. I open it to find Eliza standing there, a six-pack of beer in one hand and a knowing smile on her face. My heart does a familiar flip in my chest.

"Thought you could use some company," she

says, brushing past me into the room. The scent of her perfume lingers, and it instantly transports me back to late-night recording sessions and stolen moments on tour buses.

I can't help but smile as I close the door, grateful for the distraction from my darker thoughts. "You're a mind reader, Kerr."

She sets the beer on the desk and turns to face me, her steel-grey eyes searching my face. Her gaze flicks to the untouched mini-bar, then back to me. There's no judgment in her eyes, just understanding. "Rough night?"

I shrug, trying to play it cool even as relief washes over me at her presence. "Just the usual tour jitters. Nothing I can't handle."

Eliza raises an eyebrow, not buying it for a second. "Right. That's why you look like you're about to crawl out of your skin. Vegas bringing up some memories?"

I wince. Of course she'd know. Eliza always knows. "Yeah, you could say that."

She hands me a beer, her fingers brushing mine in a way that sends a jolt through my system. We've been doing this dance for years now, maintaining a professional relationship that's always on the edge of something more. Ever since our respective marriages imploded, there's been this unspoken thing between us, a tension that never quite goes away.

I take a long swig of beer, grateful for the familiar

burn. It's not the hard stuff from the mini-bar, but it takes the edge off. "It's just... being back here, you know? Everywhere I look, I'm reminded of that night. Of how spectacularly I fucked up."

Eliza's expression softens. She moves to sit on the edge of the bed, patting the space next to her. I hesitate for a moment before joining her, acutely aware of how close we are, of the heat radiating from her body.

"Chase," she says softly, "we all make mistakes. What matters is what we do after."

Her words wash over me, a balm to my frayed nerves. This is why I've always been drawn to Eliza. She sees me, really sees me, in a way no one else does. Not the rockstar, not the screw-up, just... me.

"I just... I don't want to let anyone down," I admit, staring at the bottle in my hands. "The band, the fans... you."

Eliza's hand comes to rest on my arm, her touch sending sparks across my skin. "The only person you need to worry about letting down is yourself. And from where I'm sitting, you're doing a pretty damn good job of being Chase Avery."

I look up, meeting her gaze. The air between us feels charged, heavy with unspoken words and suppressed desire. For a moment, I let myself remember all the times we've been here before – the almost-kisses, the lingering touches, the moments where we came so close to crossing that line.

"Eliza," I breathe, her name a prayer on my lips.

She leans in, just slightly, her eyes never leaving mine. "Chase..."

And then we're kissing, and it's like coming home and jumping off a cliff all at once. Her lips are soft against mine, tasting of beer and promises we can never quite make. My hands find her waist, pulling her closer as she threads her fingers through my hair.

For a few blissful moments, the world narrows to just this: the softness of Eliza's skin, the quiet sounds she makes as I trail kisses down her neck, the way her body fits perfectly against mine. It's familiar and new all at once, years of pent-up longing pouring out in every touch.

But reality crashes back in all too soon. We break apart, both breathing heavily. Eliza's cheeks are flushed, her hair mussed, and it takes every ounce of willpower I have not to pull her back in.

"We shouldn't," she says, but there's no conviction in her voice.

"I know," I reply, even as my body screams at me to disagree.

We sit there for a moment, the silence heavy between us. I can see the conflict in Eliza's eyes, the same war between want and responsibility that I'm fighting.

Finally, Eliza stands, smoothing down her clothes. "This doesn't have to mean anything," she says, not quite meeting my eyes. "No strings, right? Just... comfort between friends."

I nod, ignoring the ache in my chest. "Right. No strings."

As she leaves, closing the door softly behind her, I fall back on the bed, staring at the ceiling. *No strings*, we say, but I can feel them wrapping around my heart, binding me to her in ways I can't even begin to understand.

The room feels colder without her, emptier. I reach for my guitar, needing to channel this whirlwind of emotions into something tangible. As I start to play, a melody forms – bittersweet and yearning, just like us.

I know this can't last. That someday, the tightrope we're walking will snap. But for now, I'll take what I can get. Because a moment with Eliza, strings or no strings, is better than a lifetime without her.

Even if it's slowly breaking my heart.

As the notes of the new song fill the room, I can't help but wonder: how long can we keep pretending that what's between us is anything less than everything?

Don't Tell Me

ELIZA

THE MUSTY SCENT of aged paper and dust tickles my nose as I push open the attic door. Shafts of late afternoon sunlight cut through the gloom, illuminating dancing motes in the air. I sneeze, the sound echoing in the cramped space.

"Get it together, Eliza," I mutter to myself. "You're the President of Blackmore Records, not some sentimental schoolgirl."

But as I pull down the box marked *'Incendiary Ink - Early Years,'* my hands are trembling. I settle onto the dusty floor, realizing my white jeans were a bad idea as I look at the years of dust around me. Professional Eliza would be horrified. But right now, I can't bring myself to care.

The first item I pull out is a demo CD, its case cracked and label faded. I close my eyes, transported back to the first time I heard Chase's raw, powerful voice coming through my office speakers. I'd known then, in that moment, that I'd discovered something special.

Next comes a stack of contracts, my own neat handwriting in the margins. Notes like "Negotiate publishing rights" and "Discuss tour budget" remind me of late nights poring over legal documents, fighting to get the best deal for a band I believed in with every fiber of my being.

A small velvet pouch falls out as I move the contracts aside. I open it, and a guitar pick falls into my palm. It's worn and slightly chipped, with "CA" etched into one side. The memory hits me like a physical blow.

Austin, Texas. July 2005. Chase, high on the energy of a killer show, jumping off the stage and pressing the pick into my hand. His fingers lingering on mine, his eyes bright with something more than just post-performance adrenaline. "Couldn't have done it without you, Eliza," he'd said, his voice husky. It had taken every ounce of willpower not to kiss him right there.

I close my fist around the pick, the edges digging into my palm. Remembering another special guitar pick… *This is dangerous territory, Eliza. Remember - professional boundaries.*

But as I continue to sift through the box, those boundaries become increasingly blurred. Concert tickets and passes from shows I'd watched from the wings, my heart swelling with pride. Handwritten notes from Chase, usually scribbled on hotel stationery - some professional, some decidedly not.

I pull out a photo album, its edges worn from frequent handling. I flip it open, and there we are - the band and me, all impossibly young and full of hope. There's Will, grinning widely behind his drum kit. Mark, guitar slung low, trying to look cool but unable to hide his excitement. And Chase... God, Chase.

His eyes are bright with that fire I'd recognized from the first moment I saw him perform. I trace the line of his jaw with my finger, remembering how it felt under my lips in stolen moments on tour buses and in dimly lit hotel rooms. The ghost of his touch sends a shiver down my spine, and I snap the album shut.

"Focus, Eliza," I scold myself. "You're here to write a speech, not moon over ancient history."

But as I reach for my laptop, another item catches my eye. A small, leather-bound journal, tucked away at the bottom of the box. With trembling hands, I open it to a random page:

September 3, 2007 - Board meeting today about Incendiary Ink's third album budget. Had to fight tooth and nail for the resources they need. Sometimes I wonder if the other execs see what I see in them. In him. Chase played me a new song after the meeting. Said it was a thank you for always having their backs. There's a line in the chorus that keeps repeating in my head: 'In the silence between words, there's a truth we've never heard.' I can't help but wonder if he's trying to tell me something. Or am I just projecting my own feelings? This is dangerous territory, Eliza. The band needs you as a manager, not a lovesick groupie.

I close my eyes, remembering that day vividly. The frustration of the meeting, the triumph of winning the budget battle, and then... Chase. The way his voice had softened on certain lines, the intensity in his gaze as he watched for my reaction. That song eventually became *Whispered Truths*, and hearing it at the rehearsal had nearly broken me.

As I sit there, surrounded by the physical evidence of a lifetime of almosts and not-quites, I realize something. This speech isn't just about inducting Incendiary Ink into the Hall of Fame. It's about acknowledging a fundamental truth I've been running from for years.

Chase Avery didn't just change the face of rock music. He changed me. And maybe it's finally time I admitted that - to myself, to him, and to the world.

But as I reach for my laptop, ready to pour my heart out, my phone buzzes. It's an email from the board, reminding me of the need for "professionalism and objectivity" in the induction speech. The real world comes crashing back in, and I'm suddenly very aware of the dust on my clothes and the lateness of the hour.

I stand, brushing myself off, trying to shake away the lingering emotions. I have a responsibility to the company, to the band, to maintain professional boundaries.

But as I descend from the attic, the guitar pick clutched tightly in my hand, I can't help but wonder: At what cost?

I sit at my desk, open a new document, and type:

Ladies and gentlemen, let me tell you about the band that didn't just make music - they made history. Let me tell you about Incendiary Ink.

The words begin to flow, professional and polished. But underneath each carefully crafted sentence lurks the truth I can't fully express. The story of a woman who found herself while shepherding a band to stardom. The story of a love that never quite was, but never quite wasn't.

As I write deep into the night, I realize that this speech, like my relationship with Chase, will be an exercise in walking a tightrope. Professional, but personal. Revealing, but restrained.

Just like always.

June 15, 2014

The champagne flows freely, the sound of laughter and clinking glasses filling the opulent ballroom of the Beverly Hills Hotel. Incendiary Ink's 10th anniversary with Blackmore Records is in full swing, and I can't help but feel a surge of pride as I watch the band mingle with industry bigwigs.

My eyes, as always, are drawn to Chase. He's holding court near the bar, his charisma palpable even from across the room. Our eyes meet, and he gives me a subtle wink that sends a shiver down my spine. Eight months of secret rendezvous, stolen kisses, and nights that leave me breathless flash through my mind.

I excuse myself from a conversation with some executives and weave my way towards a quiet balcony, knowing Chase will follow. Sure enough, moments later, I hear his familiar footsteps behind me.

"Quite a party, Ms. Kerr," he says, his voice low

and playful. "You really know how to celebrate a decade of putting up with us."

I turn to face him, unable to suppress my smile. "Well, Mr. Avery, you've made it worth my while."

The double meaning hangs in the air between us, filled with the electricity that's always there. Chase steps closer, his fingers brushing mine in a touch that's both innocent and deeply intimate.

"I have something for you," I say, reaching into my clutch. "A little token of appreciation."

I pull out a small velvet box and hand it to him. Chase's eyebrows raise in surprise as he opens it, revealing a stainless steel guitar pick. On one side, our initials "CA" and "EK" are engraved. He flips it over, reading aloud the words on the other side:

Through every chord and silence, I'm here.

Chase looks up at me, his green eyes intense with an emotion I'm afraid to name. "Eliza," he breathes, "this is... thank you."

Before I can respond, he's pulling me into a secluded corner of the balcony, his lips crashing into mine with a hunger that matches my own. I melt into him, propriety forgotten as his hands roam my body, familiar yet thrilling.

"My room," I gasp between kisses. "Now."

The elevator ride is torturous, the need to maintain appearances at odds with our desperate desire

As soon as my suite door closes behind us, the air changes. The playful tension from earlier crystallizes into something more intense, more urgent. Chase's eyes darken as they roam over me, and I feel my breath catch in my throat.

"Eliza," he breathes, my name a plea on his lips. He closes the distance between us in two long strides, his hands cradling my face as if I'm something precious, breakable.

The first kiss is soft, almost reverent. But as I thread my fingers through his hair, pulling him closer, the dam breaks. Suddenly, we're a tangle of limbs and half-removed clothing, desperation fueling our movements.

Chase presses me against the wall, his lips blazing a trail down my neck. Each touch, each kiss feels like he's trying to memorize me, to burn this moment into his memory. "God, Eliza," he murmurs against my skin, "what you do to me... I've never felt this way with anyone else."

His words send a shiver through me, equal parts exhilaration and fear. I pull him closer, trying to lose myself in the feel of his body against mine. "Show me," I challenge, my voice husky with desire and something deeper, something I'm afraid to name.

What follows is a symphony of passion, our bodies moving together in perfect harmony. But it's more than just physical; there's an emotional intimacy that terrifies and exhilarates me in equal measure.

As Chase moves above me, his eyes never leaving mine, I feel exposed in a way that has nothing to do with our lack of clothing. It's as if he can see right through me, past all my carefully constructed walls, to the part of me that's always been his.

"Chase," I gasp, overwhelmed by the intensity of it all. He seems to understand without words, his movements becoming more purposeful, more focused.

"I've got you," he murmurs, his voice thick with emotion. "Let go, Eliza. I've got you."

And I do. For a moment, I let myself believe that this could be more than what it is, that we could have more than stolen moments and secret rendezvous. As we fall over the edge together, Chase's name on my lips and mine on his, I feel a sense of completeness I've never experienced before.

Afterwards, we lie tangled in the sheets, our breathing slowly returning to normal. Chase idly traces patterns on my skin, and I fight the urge to purr like a contented cat. The guitar pick glints on the nightstand, a tangible reminder of the unspoken thing between us.

"Eliza," Chase says softly, breaking the comfortable silence. "What are we doing?"

And just like that, reality comes crashing back in.

I tense, knowing this conversation was inevitable but dreading it, nonetheless. "We're celebrating a successful decade," I deflect weakly.

Chase props himself up on an elbow, looking down at me with those piercing eyes. "You know that's not what I mean. This... us. It's more than just our 'no strings' arrangement, isn't it?"

I sit up, clutching the sheet to my chest like a shield. "Chase, we can't... I can't..."

"Why not?" he presses gently. "Eliza, what we have... it's special. You have to feel it too."

I close my eyes, fighting back tears. Of course I feel it. How could I not? But the memory of two failed marriages looms large, and the thought of risking my heart – and potentially my son's stability – terrifies me.

"I do feel it," I admit quietly. "But Chase, I'm not... I can't be ready for that. Not even with you. Especially not with you."

The words hang in the air for a moment, and I can almost hear something snap inside Chase. His eyes flash with a sudden, fierce anger that makes me flinch.

"Especially not me?" he repeats, his voice low and dangerous. He pulls away from me, standing up abruptly. "What the hell is that supposed to mean, Eliza?"

I sit up, clutching the sheet to my chest, suddenly feeling very exposed. "Chase, I didn't mean—"

"No, let's hear it," he cuts me off, pacing the room like a caged animal. "Am I not good enough for you? After everything we've been through, everything we've shared, I'm still just the screwed-up rockstar you need to keep at arm's length?"

His words sting, but I can hear the hurt beneath the anger. "That's not fair, Chase. You know that's not what I meant."

He whirls to face me, his eyes blazing. "Then what did you mean? Because from where I'm standing, it sounds like you're saying I'm good enough to fuck, but not good enough to love."

I gasp, shocked by his crudeness. "Chase!"

"No, Eliza," he says, his voice cracking with desperation now. "I need to understand. What is it about me that makes me so unworthy of taking a chance on? Is it the drinking? Because I'm working on that. The commitment issues? I'm here, aren't I? Trying to have this conversation?"

He drops to his knees beside the bed, grabbing my hands in his. "Tell me what I need to do, Eliza. Tell me how to be the man you can trust with your heart. Because I'm drowning here, trying to figure out how to be enough for you."

The raw vulnerability in his voice makes my heart ache. I cup his face in my hands, forcing him to look at me. "Chase, listen to me. You are enough. You've always been enough. That's what scares me."

He looks confused, so I continue, "I've built my whole life around being strong, independent. But with you... God, Chase, with you, I feel like I could lose myself completely. And I'm terrified of what that would mean for me, for my career, for Justin. And then there's the band, and my responsibility there... There's too many other factors to consider here, and you know it."

Understanding dawns in his eyes, the anger melting away. "Eliza," he says softly, "loving someone doesn't mean losing yourself. It means finding a partner to face life with."

I feel tears sliding down my cheeks. "I want to believe that. I do. But I've been burned before, Chase. We both have."

He nods, pressing his forehead to mine. "I know. And I know I've given you plenty of reasons to doubt me in the past. But Eliza, I'm here now. Really here. And I'm not going anywhere."

For a moment, I let myself imagine it. A life with Chase, navigating the complexities of our careers and my role as a mother, but doing it together. It's a beautiful vision, but the fear still gnaws at me.

"And what about the band?" I ask, trying my best to paint the full picture for him. Trying to make him understand how complicated this truly is. "What if we get together, and it ruins everything we've all worked so hard for?"

He jumps up again, his emotions a whirlwind. "Then I'll quit the fucking band. Some things are more important--"

"No," I interrupt, sitting up and grabbing his arm to get his full attention. The fears I've ignored are now on plain view to him. "That's exactly what I'm talking about. Exactly what I'm afraid of."

"But, Eliza..."

"No, Chase. We have so many other things to consider. So many other people to consider. People depending on us to keep things afloat. We can't risk all of that on a maybe. And that's what we are, Chase. We're an unknown. An unknown we can't gamble on. Not with so much at stake." My voice is hoarse with emotion. I know this is the right thing to do, but it's killing me to say it so bluntly like this. And the hurt on his face is like a mirror to my own, as he nods his defeat.

God, what I would give to let myself go with him. Just ignore responsibility for a change and let myself be truly happy. Because I would be. I know I would be happy. But I also know that the two of us together would have ripple effects that we don't even know about, and I can't take that chance. Not now.

Maybe not ever.

He comes back to bed, his chilled skin setting mine ablaze as he runs his fingers down my spine, making me shiver against him.

"Okay. I get it," he concedes, searching my eyes with so much hope it hurts my heart. "But don't take it completely off the table, okay? Can you promise me that much?"

"I need time," I whisper, giving what truth I can in

the moment. "I can't promise you anything right now, Chase. Can you understand that?"

He's quiet for a long moment, and I can see him wrestling with his emotions. Finally, he nods. "I don't like it," he admits. "But I understand. And Eliza? I'll wait. As long as it takes."

"Don't say that," I say sadly, half choking on the words as I push the hair out of his brilliant eyes. The idea of him waiting for me is almost as painful as everything else. This isn't fair to him. And it's not fair to me either. We're both losers in this. I'm okay with being alone. I can live with hard decisions like this, but Chase? I don't think he can, and it scares the shit out of me what this could do to him. "Just, please don't."

He studies me closely, and he must finally realize what I'm truly saying. I can't hold back my tears that slowly fall down my cheeks. Tears that I've shed in private for so long, now on full display. Tears for a life together we'll never have. For the dream that keeps me up at night, knowing it will never be real. For the hard choices I continually have to make.

I'm tired of being the strong one. The one who sacrifices everything for everyone else. It's soul exhausting, and I'm barely hanging on by a thread. The dam breaks, and I curl up into sobs, barely catching my breath.

Chase pulls me into his strong arms, not saying a word, just holding me close as I release every emotion. He softly kisses my cheeks, my forehead, my hair, pulling me tighter to him as I fight the war within myself. Internally raging at the world for being so unfair, and shrinking in defeat from the battle between my heart and my head that I've lost miserably. Logical me has won again, and I hate it. I fucking loathe it.

I eventually fall asleep in his arms, but when I awake in the middle of the night with Chase asleep beside me, I find myself staring at the guitar pick on the nightstand. *Through every chord and silence, I'm here*, I'd promised him. But as I lie awake, I wonder if being here, like this, is enough. Or if it's slowly breaking both our hearts.

Because mine is absolutely shattered.

Speechless

CHASE

THE FAMILIAR SCENT of old amps and stale coffee greets me as I push open the door to our rehearsal space. It's been our sanctuary for years, but today it feels different. Charged. Important.

Will and Mark are already here, lounging on the battered leather couch that's seen better days. They both look up as I enter, matching grins on their faces.

"Look who finally decided to grace us with his presence," Will quips, but there's no heat in it.

I'm about to retort when the door opens again, and my words die in my throat. Eliza walks in, looking every inch the powerful executive in her tailored suit. It must be a board meeting day. Our eyes meet, and for a moment, I'm transported back to every stolen glance, every secret touch we've shared over the years.

But, she's not alone. Ryan Crawford from Indigo

King follows, his easy smile and tousled dark hair a stark contrast to Eliza's polished appearance. Behind him is Jude Lockwood, Indigo King's bassist, his tall frame slouching as if trying to take up less space. And finally, Jake Townsend of Murderous Crows, his long blonde hair tied back, eyes darting around the room as if mapping escape routes. We all know each other, having toured together multiple times, so no introductions are needed, and fist bumps and handshakes make their rounds.

"Gentlemen," Eliza says, her voice steady and professional. "Thank you for meeting us here. We have some details to discuss about the induction ceremony."

As everyone settles in, I can't help but notice the slight tremor in Eliza's hands as she opens her folder. It's barely noticeable, but I've known her long enough to recognize when she's unsettled.

"So," Jude drawls, breaking the silence, "are we here to worship at the altar of Incendiary Ink, or what?"

Will snorts. "Please, like you're not honored to be in our presence."

"Boys," Eliza interjects, a hint of amusement in her voice. "Let's focus. We have a lot to cover."

She outlines the plan for the ceremony, and I find myself leaning forward, hanging on every word. The three songs we talked about, but not individually. A medley. Other bands playing along with us in tribute. It's exciting, but also overwhelming.

"The speeches will actually be longer than the performances," Eliza explains. "Chase, that means you'll need to prepare something substantial."

I nod, my mind already racing. What can I possibly say that will encompass everything this band has meant to me? Everything Eliza has meant to me?

"Jake," Eliza continues, turning to the quiet frontman of Murderous Crows, "we were hoping you'd take the lead on *Whispered Truths* during the medley."

"Wait, what?" I interrupt, surprised by the force in my own voice. Everyone turns to look at me. "I mean... shouldn't I be singing that one? It's kind of... personal."

Eliza's eyes meet mine, and for a moment, her professional facade cracks. I see a flicker of something – understanding? Longing? – before she composes herself. "We thought it might be nice to have a tribute element," she says, her voice slightly strained. "But if you feel strongly about it..."

"I do," I say firmly. "That song... it needs to come from me."

The room is silent for a moment, the tension palpable. Finally, Jake speaks up, his voice soft but clear. "I think Chase is right. It wouldn't feel right, singing that one." He pauses, then adds, "How about I take *Burning Bridges* instead? That song's always resonated with me."

I feel a rush of gratitude towards Jake. *Burning Bridges* is a powerful song, but it doesn't carry the same emotional weight for me as *Whispered Truths*.

Eliza nods, and I see her swallow hard before speaking. "That's a great suggestion, Jake. We'll adjust the arrangement accordingly."

As the meeting continues, we dive into the nitty-gritty of the performance. Ryan and Jude chime in with ideas for harmonies and instrumental breaks, their excitement palpable. It's surreal, hearing our music dissected and reimagined by these talented musicians.

Throughout it all, I find my attention continually drawn to Eliza. She's in her element, commanding the room with an ease that never fails to impress me. But there's something else too – a tension in her shoulders, a tightness around her eyes that only someone who knows her as well as I do would notice.

When there's a lull in the conversation, I seize my chance. "Eliza, can I talk to you for a second? About the song arrangements?"

She hesitates for just a moment before nodding. "Of course. Let's step outside."

In the hallway, the professional facade Eliza's been maintaining cracks slightly. "Chase," she says, her voice softer now, "what's this really about?"

I take a deep breath. "I just... I wanted to make

sure you're okay with all of this. The song choices, the memories they're bringing up. I know it can't be easy."

Something flickers in her eyes before she tries to school her features. But this time, I see the cracks in her armor. Her voice wavers slightly as she speaks. "It's... it's fine, Chase. This is about the band, about your legacy. My feelings don't factor into it."

"But they do," I insist gently. "At least to me, they do."

Eliza sighs, running a hand through her hair in a rare display of vulnerability. "Chase, please. We can't... we've been over this."

I want to argue, to tell her that maybe it's time we stopped pretending, stopped hiding behind professionalism and caution. But before I can say anything, the door opens and Will pokes his head out.

"Everything okay out here?" he asks, his eyes darting between Eliza and me.

Eliza straightens, trying to slip her professional mask back into place, but I can see the cracks now. "Everything's fine. We were just discussing some final details about the performance."

As we head back into the rehearsal space, I can't shake the feeling that we're at a crossroads. The induction ceremony looms ahead, promising to dredge up years of history, of feelings we've both tried to bury.

And as I watch Eliza dive back into planning

mode, expertly navigating the egos and ideas in the room, I realize something. No matter what happens on that stage, no matter what words I say in my speech, the real performance will be this – Eliza and me, pretending that what's between us is anything less than everything.

But as Jake starts to sing the opening lines of *Burning Bridges,* his haunting voice filling the room, I make a silent promise to myself. This time, I won't let our story end in ashes. This time, I'll find a way to bridge the gap between us, no matter what it takes.

February 8, 2015

The Staples Center thrums with an energy that's almost palpable. I adjust my tie for the thousandth time, the designer suit feeling both foreign and empowering. Will nudges me, a grin splitting his face.

"Dude, stop fidgeting. We look good."

I manage a smile, but my stomach is in knots. We're up for three awards tonight: Best Rock Performance, Best Rock Song, and the big one - Best Rock Album. It's surreal, being here among the glitterati of the music world.

My eyes scan the crowd, inevitably drawn to her. Eliza sits a few rows ahead, looking stunning in a deep blue gown that makes her blonde hair shine like spun white gold. She turns, as if sensing my gaze, and gives me a small smile and nod. My heart does a familiar flip, and I have to remind myself: *she knows how you feel. She's made her choice. You need to move on.*

The ceremony passes in a blur of performances and awards. When they announce "Best Rock Performance," and our name is called, everything seems to move in slow motion. We're on our feet, hugging each other, and suddenly I'm moving down the aisle.

Without thinking, driven by pure adrenaline and joy, I stop at Eliza's row. Her eyes widen in surprise as I lean down and plant a quick, excited kiss on her lips. It's over in a second, but the shock of it reverberates through me as I continue to the stage.

As I approach the mic, my bandmates clustered around me, I'm acutely aware of what I've just done. But the euphoria of the win overshadows everything else. The words tumble out, thanking our families, our team, our fans.

And then I see Eliza in the audience, her fingers touching her lips, a mix of emotions playing across her face. I can't help myself.

"And finally," I say, my voice thick with emotion, "I want to thank someone who's been with us from the very beginning. Eliza Kerr, our manager, our rock. Without you, we wouldn't be standing here today. You saw something in us when no one else did, and you never stopped believing. This is as much yours as it is ours."

The applause swells, and as we're ushered offstage, I catch a glimpse of Eliza's face. She's blinking rapidly, clearly fighting back tears.

The night continues, a whirlwind of interviews and congratulations. We win Best Rock Song, and then, in a moment that feels like a dream, Best Rock Album.

This time, when I take the mic, I'm more composed. I talk about the journey of making the album, the late nights and creative struggles. But once again, I find my gaze drawn to Eliza.

"You know, they say behind every great band is a great manager. But Eliza Kerr isn't behind us - she's beside us, in front of us, showing us the way forward. She's the unsung hero of Incendiary Ink, and I want the world to know it."

The afterparty is a riot of celebration. Champagne flows freely, and everywhere I turn, there's another hand to shake, another back to pat. But through it all, I'm aware of Eliza's presence, both drawn to her and trying to maintain a respectful distance.

I finally spot her near the bar, deep in conversation with some industry bigwig. She excuses herself when she sees me approach, and for a moment, we just stand there, an awkward tension between us.

"Congratulations, Chase," she says softly. "You deserve this. All of it."

"We deserve this," I correct her. "I meant what I said up there, Eliza. We wouldn't be here without you." I pause, then add, "About earlier... I'm sorry if I overstepped. I got caught up in the moment."

Something flickers in her eyes – longing, maybe? -- before she masks it with a professional smile. "It's okay. It was... unexpected, but I understand. It's an emotional night."

I want to say more, to reignite the conversation about us, about what we could be. But I've said it all before, and I know where we stand. Instead, I raise my champagne glass. "To Incendiary Ink, and the best manager in the business."

Eliza clinks her glass against mine, her eyes never leaving mine. "To Incendiary Ink, and the most talented frontman I've ever worked with."

The moment is broken by Will, slinging an arm around my shoulders. "Come on, man! They want pictures with the Grammy winners!"

As I'm pulled away, I look back at Eliza. She gives me a small wave, a mix of emotions playing across her face.

Later that night, as I fall into bed, still in my rumpled suit with three Grammy awards on the night-stand, my phone buzzes. It's a text from Eliza:

ELIZA: I'm proud of you, Chase.
Always have been, always will be.

I stare at the message, a bittersweet ache filling

me. Three Grammy awards, and yet the thing I want most still feels just out of reach. I know I need to try to move on, to accept that what Eliza and I have might never be more than what it is now. But nights like this make it so damn hard.

> ME: Couldn't have done it without you. Thank you for everything, Eliza.

As I hit send, I make a silent promise to myself. I'll keep trying to move forward, to find happiness beyond this complicated relationship. But a part of me will always hope that someday, somehow, Eliza and I will find our way to each other.

For now, though, I'll savor this moment. It's not everything I want, but it's pretty damn amazing all the same.

Better Days

ELIZA

THE LATE AFTERNOON sun beats down on us as I heave another box out of the moving truck. Justin's newly renovated house looms before me, a testament to my son's success and independence. A success that, I can't help but think, came in spite of his tumultuous upbringing.

"Easy there, Liz," a gravelly voice calls out. "Don't strain yourself. We wouldn't want the big-shot record exec to throw her back out."

I turn to see Jimmy sauntering towards me, a smirk playing on his lips. James Montague, my ex-husband and Justin's father, still carries himself with the swagger of the rockstar he always thought he'd be. The years haven't been particularly kind – his once-chiseled features are now weathered, lined with the evidence of hard living. But there's still a glimmer of that charm that once swept me off my feet.

"I can manage just fine, Jimmy," I retort, hefting the box higher. "Some of us actually stayed in shape past thirty."

Justin appears between us, his eyes darting nervously from me to his father. "Mom, Dad, please. Can we not do this today?"

Guilt washes over me. This is Justin's day, and here we are, falling into old patterns. "You're right, honey. I'm sorry."

Jimmy has the grace to look abashed. "Yeah, sorry, kid. Old habits, you know?"

We make our way into the house, depositing boxes in their designated rooms. As we work, I can't help but notice the way Jimmy's hands shake slightly as he sets down a stack of books. The telltale signs of a life lived hard and fast.

"So, Eliza," Jimmy says as we take a water break in the kitchen, "heard your boys are getting inducted into the Hall of Fame. Must be nice, having a success story under your belt."

There's an edge to his words that I choose to ignore. "They've worked hard for it. They deserve the recognition."

Jimmy snorts. "Yeah, I bet. Especially that lead singer of theirs. What's his name again? Chase?"

I stiffen involuntarily at the mention of Chase's name. Jimmy, ever observant despite his faults, doesn't miss it.

"Hit a nerve, did I?" he prods. "You always did have a soft spot for the pretty boy rockers."

"Dad," Justin interjects, his voice sharp. "That's enough."

I take a deep breath, forcing myself to relax. "Chase and the whole band have been incredible to work with. Their success is their own."

As I say it, I can't help but think of Chase – his dedication, his talent, the way he's grown not just as an artist but as a person. The contrast between him and Jimmy is stark, a before-and-after of two very different paths in the music industry.

Jimmy must see something in my expression because his next words are uncharacteristically soft. "You did good with them, Liz. Always knew you had it in you to be something special in this business."

The compliment, rare as it is, catches me off guard. "Thanks, Jimmy," I manage, a lump forming in my throat.

Justin looks between us, a mix of surprise and hope on his face. It's moments like these that remind me why I've tried to maintain a civil relationship with Jimmy all these years – for our son's sake.

As the day wears on, the bickering resurfaces occasionally, but there's less heat behind it. We order pizza for dinner, and as we sit on boxes in Justin's half-furnished living room, I find myself reflecting on the journey that brought us here.

Jimmy, for all his faults, did try in his own way.

He might not have been the father Justin deserved, but he was the one who showed up, even if it was sporadically. And watching them now, sharing a laugh over some old family story, I feel a complicated mix of emotions – regret for what could have been, gratitude for what is, and a strange sort of peace with how things turned out.

As I'm leaving for the night, Justin pulls me into a tight hug. "Thanks, Mom. For everything."

I hold him close, marveling at the man he's become. "Always, sweetheart. I'm so proud of you."

Jimmy, hovering awkwardly nearby, clears his throat. "You did good with him too, Liz. He's a great kid."

"We did okay," I concede, offering Jimmy a small smile.

Driving home, I find my thoughts drifting to Chase, to the upcoming induction ceremony. I think about the man he is now compared to the young rocker I first met. I think about Jimmy, about the paths not taken and the choices that shape a life.

My phone buzzes with a text from Chase.

> CHASE: How's the moving day going? Need any help?

I smile, warmth spreading through me at his thoughtfulness.

> ME: All done. Thanks for offering.
> See you at rehearsal tomorrow?

His reply is almost instant.

> CHASE: Wouldn't miss it.
> Goodnight, Eliza.

As I pull into my driveway, I'm struck by a realization. Life rarely turns out the way we expect. Jimmy and I crashed and burned, but we created Justin. Chase and I... well, that story is still being written.

And for the first time in a long time, I find myself looking forward to the next chapter.

September 15, 2017

The setting sun paints Chase's Malibu home in hues of gold and orange as I pull into the driveway. My hands tremble as I turn off the engine, the weight of the impending conversation sitting like lead in my stomach. The folder on the passenger seat seems to mock me – filled with corporate jargon that can't begin to encompass what this decision really means.

I've rehearsed this a thousand times, but now, staring at the front door, all my carefully prepared words evaporate. How do you tell someone who's been the cornerstone of your career, your life, for over a decade that you're stepping away?

Before I can knock, the door swings open. Chase stands there, backlit by the warm glow of his home, a broad smile on his face that makes my heart fracture just a little more.

"Eliza!" he exclaims, genuine joy in his voice. "I wasn't expecting you. Come in, come in."

I follow him into the living room, trying to ignore how at home I feel here. The air is thick with the scent of coffee and that distinctive Chase smell – a mix of sandalwood and something uniquely him. Guitars are propped against walls, notebooks filled with his messy scrawl litter every surface. It's organized chaos, just like the man himself.

"Can I get you something to drink?" he asks, already heading towards the kitchen. "I've got that pinot noir you like."

The casual intimacy of knowing my favorite wine hits me hard. "No, I'm fine," I manage, my voice strained. "Chase, we need to talk."

He turns, his brow furrowing at my tone. "Okay... that sounds ominous. What's up?"

I take a deep breath, steeling myself. "I've been offered a promotion. Vice President of Blackmore Records."

For a moment, his face lights up, pride and excitement shining in his eyes. "Eliza, that's amazing!

Congratulations! We should celebrate, I'll open that champagne we've been saving-"

"Chase," I interrupt, each word feeling like glass in my throat. "There's more."

He stops, the bottle halfway out of the wine fridge. I watch as understanding dawns on his face, followed quickly by hurt, then a flash of anger he tries to mask.

"They want you to stop managing us," he says flatly. It's not a question.

I nod, unable to form the words. The silence stretches between us, heavy with unspoken history.

Chase sets the bottle down with deliberate care. When he looks at me again, his eyes are guarded. "So, after everything, you're just... walking away?"

"It's not like that," I argue, even as a voice in my head whispers that maybe it is. "This is a huge opportunity, Chase. For me, for the label... it could mean big things for the band too."

He laughs, but it's a harsh sound, nothing like the warm chuckle I've grown to love. "Right. Because some new manager is going to understand us, understand our vision, the way you do. The way you always have."

I feel tears pricking at the corners of my eyes. "Chase, please. Try to understand. This isn't easy for me either."

"Then don't do it," he says, his voice suddenly soft, pleading. He steps closer, and I catch a whiff of his cologne – the same one he wore the night we first kissed. "We need you, Eliza. I need you."

For a moment, I waver. The pull between us, the connection we've always had, it's strong enough to make me consider throwing it all away. But then I think of all the late nights, the sacrifices, the years I've poured into getting to this point.

"I'm sorry," I whisper, the words tasting bitter. "I have to do this. For me."

Something shutters in Chase's eyes, and he steps back as if I've physically struck him. "Right. For you. Well, congratulations on the promotion, Ms. Kerr. I'm sure you'll do great things."

The formality stings more than outright anger would have. "Chase..."

"You know," he interrupts, his voice low and intense, "I always thought that when it came down to it, you'd choose us. Choose me. Like I would have chosen you. Every time."

His words hit me like a physical blow. "It's not about choosing, Chase. It's about growth. Change."

"Change," he repeats, the word dripping with sarcasm. "Is that what we're calling it now? Because from where I'm standing, it looks a lot like running away."

Anger flares in me, hot and sudden. "That's not fair. I've given everything to this band, to you, for years. I've put my life on hold, my relationships-"

"Our relationship, you mean?" Chase cuts in, his

eyes flashing. "The one we've been dancing around for over a decade? The one you've always kept at arm's length because it wasn't 'professional'?"

I flinch, the truth of his words cutting deep. "That's... that's not what this is about."

"Isn't it?" he challenges. "Because it seems to me that every time we get close to something real, you find a way to put more distance between us. And now this."

Tears are flowing freely now, and I make no effort to stop them. "Chase, please. This is my career, my future. Can't you understand that?"

For a moment, the anger seems to drain out of him, replaced by a bone-deep weariness. "I understand that you're making a choice, Eliza. I just wish, for once, that choice had been me."

The finality in his voice terrifies me. "This doesn't have to be the end," I say, hating how desperate I sound. "I'll still be involved with the label, we'll still see each other-"

"It won't be the same," he says quietly. "You know it won't."

And I do know. With crushing certainty, I realize that this moment, this decision, is changing everything between us.

"I should go," I murmur, unable to bear the weight of his gaze any longer.

Chase nods, turning away. "Yeah, you should. I'm sure you have a lot to prepare for in your new role."

I make my way to the door on unsteady legs, feeling as though I'm leaving a part of myself behind. As I reach for the handle, Chase speaks again, his voice so low I almost miss it.

"I hope it's worth it, Eliza. I really do."

The drive home is a blur, tears clouding my vision. I've achieved what I've always dreamed of, taken a huge step forward in my career. So why does it feel like I've lost something irreplaceable?

As I pull into my driveway, my phone buzzes with a text from Chase.

> CHASE: When are you telling the rest of the band?

I stare at the message, feeling the finality of it all crashing down on me. This is really happening. I'm really stepping away. Am I doing the right thing?

With shaking fingers, I type out a reply.

> ME: Tomorrow. Band meeting at 2.

His response is immediate and cuts me to the core.

> CHASE: I'll be there. Strictly professional from now on, right? Isn't that what you've always wanted?

I don't respond. Can't respond. Instead, I let the

tears fall freely, mourning for what feels like the end of something beautiful, even if it never fully belonged to me.

Tomorrow, I'll put on my professional face. I'll break the news to the band, weather their reactions, start the process of handing over the reins. I'll step into my new role with confidence and determination.

But tonight, I allow myself to grieve for the chapter of my life that's closing. For the relationship with Chase that, despite our best efforts to keep it professional, was always so much more.

And as I fall into a fitful sleep, Chase's words echo in my mind: *"Strictly professional."* If only it were that simple. If only it ever had been.

The Dam

CHASE

THE TICKING OF DR. HENDRICKS' antique clock seems louder than usual today. I've been staring at it for the past five minutes, watching the second hand make its relentless journey, anything to avoid the question hanging in the air.

"Chase," Dr. Hendricks' voice is gentle but firm, "you mentioned that you've been feeling tempted lately. Can you elaborate on that?"

I drag my gaze away from the clock, forcing myself to meet his eyes. "It's not... I haven't..." I take a deep breath, start again. "I haven't slipped. But God, I've wanted to."

Dr. Hendricks nods, encouraging me to continue.

"It's all this Hall of Fame stuff," I say, the words tumbling out now. "Seeing Eliza again, rehearsing the old songs... it's bringing up a lot of memories. Good ones, sure, but the bad ones too. The ones I used to drink to forget."

"And how are you handling those memories now, without the alcohol?"

I laugh, but there's no humor in it. "Not great, doc. That's why I'm here, isn't it?"

He doesn't rise to my sarcasm. Instead, he asks, "Have you been using any of the coping mechanisms we've discussed?"

I shift uncomfortably. "Some. The breathing exercises help a bit. But it's hard to step away and do that in the middle of a rehearsal, you know?"

"What about reaching out to your support system? Friends, family?"

I wince. "You know I'm not great at that, doc. It feels... I don't know, weak somehow. Like I should be able to handle this on my own by now."

Dr. Hendricks leans forward slightly. "Chase, recovery isn't about doing it alone. It's about learning to lean on others when you need to. That's strength, not weakness."

I nod, not entirely convinced but not willing to argue the point.

"Let's talk about the letter to Eliza," Dr. Hendricks changes tack. "Have you made any progress on that?"

Another wince. "Not really. I've started it a dozen times, but... how do you apologize for years of hurt in a single letter?"

"Perhaps the letter isn't meant to encompass

everything. It could be a starting point, an opening for a deeper conversation."

I consider this. "Maybe. But then there's the acceptance speech too. I'm supposed to sum up our entire career, our entire journey, in what? Five minutes?"

"It sounds like you're feeling overwhelmed," Dr. Hendricks observes. "Like you're trying to solve everything at once."

"Yeah," I admit. "I guess I am."

"Let's break this down," he suggests. "First, your recovery. What specific moments or memories have been triggering the urge to drink?"

I close my eyes, thinking. "There's this one part in *Burning Bridges* - we were rehearsing it the other day. I wrote it when I was at a real, just before one of my rehabs. Hearing it now... it's like I can taste the whiskey on my tongue again."

Dr. Hendricks nods. "And how did you handle that moment?"

"I pushed through," I say. "Finished the song. But afterwards, I had to step outside, just... breathe for a while."

"That's good, Chase. You recognized the trigger and took positive action. What else?"

I think for a moment. "Eliza's perfume," I admit quietly. "It's the same one she's always worn. One whiff and I'm back in all those moments - the good and the bad."

"And how does that make you feel?"

"Nostalgic. Sad. Angry, sometimes. At myself, mostly. For all the times I messed up, all the chances I wasted."

Dr. Hendricks is quiet for a moment, letting me sit with those emotions. Then he asks, "How do the letter and the speech tie into all of this?"

I hadn't considered this connection before. "I guess... they're both about taking responsibility, aren't they? Owning up to my past, my mistakes. But also acknowledging how far I've come."

"Exactly," Dr. Hendricks nods. "They're not separate from your recovery journey - they're part of it. So, let's start with the letter. Instead of trying to apologize for everything, what's the one thing you most want Eliza to know?"

I don't have to think long. "That I'm grateful. For her belief in me, even when I didn't believe in myself."

"That's a powerful starting point," Dr. Hendricks says. "For the speech, perhaps instead of trying to sum up everything, you could focus on the band's journey of growth - which mirrors your own personal journey."

As we continue to discuss strategies, I feel some of the overwhelming pressure start to lift. We talk about more specific coping mechanisms I can use during rehearsals, ways to ground myself when memories become overwhelming, and how to approach the letter and speech as part of my ongoing recovery rather than separate, daunting tasks.

"Remember, Chase," Dr. Hendricks says as our time winds down, "recovery isn't a destination - it's a journey. You're not failing if you struggle. The important thing is that you keep moving forward, and that you're willing to ask for help when you need it."

I nod, feeling more grounded than I have in weeks. "Thanks, doc. I... I'll try to remember that."

As I walk to my car, I pull out my phone and open a new note. At the top, I type:

Dear Eliza, I want to start by saying thank you...

It's not much, but it's a start. And right now, that feels like enough.

On the drive home, I make a decision. I pull over and dial a number I haven't used in a while.

"Hey, Will? Yeah, it's me. Listen, I was wondering... do you have some time to grab a coffee? There's some stuff I could use a friend's ear for."

It's a small step, but as I merge back into traffic, I feel a weight lift off my shoulders. Maybe Dr. Hendricks is right. Maybe asking for help isn't weakness after all.

September 16, 2017

The pounding in my head matches the insistent knocking at the door. I groan, trying to piece together where I am and how I got here. My living room, I realize, as the world slowly comes into focus. Empty bottles litter the coffee table, and there's a guitar - my favorite Gibson - lying haphazardly on the floor.

The knocking continues, now accompanied by a familiar voice. "Chase! Open up, man. We're worried about you."

Will. Shit. The band meeting. What time is it?

I try to sit up, but a wave of nausea hits me. That's when I notice the woman sprawled on the other end of the couch, her mascara smeared, clothes disheveled. I have no memory of how she got here.

"Coming," I croak out, my voice barely recognizable. I stumble to the door, nearly tripping over an overturned amp.

When I open the door, Will's worried expression quickly turns to one of shock and disappointment. "Jesus, Chase. What the hell?"

I lean against the doorframe, trying to muster some semblance of composure. "Lost track of time. Sorry about the meeting."

Will pushes past me into the house, then stops short at the scene before him. His eyes dart from the bottles to the passed-out woman on the couch, then back to me. "Lost track of time?" he repeats, his voice a mix of anger and concern. "You've gone off the deep end, man. What's going on with you?"

The events of the past couple days come rushing back, and with them, a fresh wave of pain and anger. "Eliza," I mutter, reaching for a half-empty bottle on the nearby table. "She's leaving us."

Will snatches the bottle away, his brow furrowing. "What are you talking about? Eliza's not going anywhere."

I blink at him, confused. "But... her promotion. She said..."

"If you'd been at the meeting, you'd know," Will says, his tone softening slightly. "She fought the board, Chase. Told them she wouldn't take the promotion unless she could keep managing us. She's staying on."

The news hits me like a bucket of cold water. "She... what?"

Will nods, then looks pointedly at the woman on the couch. "Who's she?"

I shrug, the movement making my head spin. "No idea. Met her at... a bar? I think?"

Will runs a hand over his face, looking suddenly tired. "Okay, here's what's going to happen. I'm going to call this woman a cab. You're going to take a shower and try to sober up. Then we're going to talk. Really talk."

I want to argue, to tell him to leave me alone, that I'm fine. But the look in his eyes - concern mixed with a steely determination - tells me it's not up for debate.

As Will helps the disoriented woman out of the house and into a cab, I drag myself to the shower. The hot water helps clear my head a little, but with clarity comes shame. What the hell am I doing?

By the time I emerge, Will has cleared away the bottles and opened some windows, letting in fresh air. He's sitting on the couch, two cups of coffee on the table in front of him.

"Sit," he says, pushing one of the mugs towards me.

I obey, the caffeine helping to further cut through the fog in my brain.

"Talk to me, Chase," Will says softly. "This isn't just about Eliza, is it?"

I bristle slightly. "What's that supposed to mean?"

Will sighs. "Come on, man. This isn't the first time you've gone on a bender. Remember after the Grammys? Or when your dad showed up out of the blue last year?"

"So I like to party sometimes," I say defensively. "We're rockstars. It's what we do."

"No," Will says firmly. "It's what *you* do. And it's getting worse, Chase. I'm worried about you."

I laugh, but there's no humor in it. "Worried? About what? I'm fine. This was just... a misunderstanding. I thought we were losing Eliza. I overreacted. It won't happen again."

Will looks at me for a long moment, like he's trying to decide whether to believe me. Finally, he nods. "Okay. But Chase? You need to talk to Eliza. She was pretty upset when you didn't show up to the meeting. She thinks you're angry with her."

Guilt washes over me. "I'll call her," I promise. "Explain everything."

"Good," Will says, standing up. "And maybe... take it easy on the drinking for a while? For all our sakes?"

I nod, even as a part of me bristles at the suggestion. I don't have a problem. I don't. This was a one-time thing.

As Will leaves, I'm left alone with my thoughts. Relief that Eliza's staying on mixes with shame over my behavior. But underneath it all, there's a nagging feeling I can't quite shake. A whisper in the back of my mind that maybe, just maybe, Will's concern isn't entirely misplaced.

I push the thought away. I'm fine. Everything's fine. And now that I know Eliza's not leaving, it will all go back to normal.

It has to.

I Am the Fire

ELIZA

I'VE JUST WRAPPED up a grueling meeting with our legal team about a 360 deal dispute with Lila Rose, our latest pop sensation. It's the kind of day-to-day work I've been neglecting in favor of Hall of Fame preparations, and the pile of tasks on my desk seems to grow exponentially.

As I settle into my ergonomic chair, my eyes drift to the framed multi-platinum plaque on my wall - Incendiary Ink's *Phoenix Rising* album. Chase's intense gaze stares back at me from the cover art, and I feel a familiar ache in my chest. I haven't been to rehearsals in over two weeks, telling myself it's because I'm swamped with work, but deep down, I know it's more than that. Every time I see Chase, every time I hear him sing, it gets harder to maintain this careful distance I've cultivated.

My intercom buzzes, jolting me from my reverie.

"Ms. Kerr? Your 2 o'clock is here. Megan Clark from Music Insider."

I take a deep breath, steeling myself. "Send her in, please."

Megan Clark breezes in, all sleek professionalism and barely concealed ambition. Her eyes dart around my office, no doubt taking in the evidence of my success - the awards, the platinum records, the photos with industry bigwigs.

"Ms. Kerr, thank you so much for making time for us," she says, her recorder already in hand. "We're thrilled to get your perspective on Incendiary Ink's induction into the Hall of Fame."

I paste on my best media smile. "Of course. It's an exciting time for the band and for Blackmore Records."

The interview starts off predictably enough. Questions about the band's journey, their impact on the industry, my role in their success. I answer on autopilot, years of media training kicking in.

"Incendiary Ink's sound evolved significantly over the years," Megan observes. "How much of that was organic growth versus label direction?"

I lean forward slightly, engaging. "It was always a collaborative process. Our job at Blackmore was to provide the resources and support for the band to explore their artistic vision. Their evolution was driven by their experiences, their growth as musicians. We just helped create the environment for that growth to happen."

Megan nods, scribbling a note. "And what about the challenges? Incendiary Ink has had their share of controversies over the years."

I choose my words carefully. "Every band faces challenges. What set Incendiary Ink apart was their resilience, their ability to channel those challenges into their music. It's part of what makes their induction so meaningful - it's a recognition not just of their success, but of their journey."

But then, Megan's smile turns slightly predatory. "Speaking of journeys, there's been a lot of speculation over the years about your personal journey with Chase Avery. Care to comment on that?"

I feel my smile freeze for a fraction of a second before I recover. "Chase and I have a long-standing professional relationship. I've been Incendiary Ink's manager since the beginning of their career."

Megan nods, but I can see she's not satisfied. "Of course. But there have been rumors of a more... intimate connection. Especially given some of Chase's more emotional acceptance speeches over the years. The Grammy incident in 2015 comes to mind."

The memory of that impulsive kiss flashes through my mind, and I have to work to keep my expression neutral. "I think it's natural for there to be a close bond between a band and their manager, especially over such a long and successful career.

Emotions can run high in moments of triumph. But I can assure you, my relationship with Chase - and with all the members of Incendiary Ink - is strictly professional."

"And yet," Megan presses, leaning forward, "sources close to the band have hinted at tensions when you considered stepping down as their manager a few years ago. Some have suggested it was more than just a professional disagreement."

I feel a flicker of anger, quickly suppressed. Who's been talking? Will? Mark? "I'm not sure what sources you're referring to, but I can tell you that any discussions about my role with the band have always been centered around what's best for their career and for Blackmore Records. The music industry is constantly evolving, and so are the roles within it."

Megan seems to sense she's pushed as far as she can. She wraps up the interview with a few more questions about the upcoming ceremony, but I can see the wheels turning behind her eyes. I know this won't be the last I hear of these rumors.

After she leaves, I sink back into my chair, suddenly drained. I thought I'd gotten better at deflecting these questions over the years, but something about this interview has left me unsettled. Is it because the ceremony is so close? Or because I've been avoiding the rehearsals, avoiding Chase?

I pull out my phone, scrolling through my recent

messages. There's one from Chase from a few days ago.

> CHASE: Missed you at rehearsal again. Everything okay? The guys are starting to think you've abandoned us. ;)

I hadn't replied. Didn't know how to without revealing too much.

As I stare at the message, Megan's words echo in my mind. Have I really been that transparent all these years? Can everyone see right through my professional facade to the complicated tangle of feelings I have for Chase?

More importantly, what am I going to do about it?

The induction ceremony is less than a month away, and with it, the prospect of standing on that stage with Chase, in front of the whole world. The thought sends a shiver down my spine - equal parts excitement and terror.

I start to type out a reply to Chase, then delete it. Then start again. Finally, I settle on:

> ME: Sorry I've been MIA. Label stuff's been crazy. Dinner this week to catch up on ceremony details?

It's not much, but it's a step. As I hit send, I can't help but wonder: how much longer can we keep dancing around this thing between us? And what happens when the music finally stops?

I guess I'll find out soon enough. For now, I have a label to run and a ceremony to prepare for. Personal feelings will have to wait. They always have. As much as I fucking hate it, I almost feel numb to it now. *Almost.*

But as I turn back to my computer, Chase's face on that album cover catches my eye again. And I wonder, not for the first time, if I'm making the biggest mistake of my life by continuing to push him away.

October 5, 2017

The throbbing bass from Chase's Malibu home vibrates through my steering wheel as I pull into the driveway. The house blazes with light, every window alive with movement and shadows. This isn't the intimate gathering I'd expected when Will mentioned a "party." This is something else entirely.

I sit for a moment, my knuckles white on the wheel. I should have come sooner. Should have talked to him right after the promotion announcement. But I'd been caught up in the whirlwind of new responsibilities, of proving to the board that I could handle both roles. And if I'm honest with myself, I'd been avoiding this conversation.

The front door stands wide open, music and voices spilling into the night. The moment I step inside, my senses are assaulted. The sickly-sweet smell of marijuana mingles with something sharper, more chemical. Cocaine. I'd recognize that smell anywhere after fifteen years in the industry. My stomach churns.

The house is packed with the kind of crowd I've spent years protecting Chase from. Dead-eyed models with hollow cheeks and twitching hands. Wannabe producers with predatory smiles. Parasites in designer clothes, all trying to get a piece of him.

Chase's beautiful Steinway grand piano, usually gleaming, is now littered with empty bottles and cigarette burns. Sheet music lies scattered across the floor, trampled and stained. This isn't a party. It's a cry for help.

I push through the crowd, years of navigating industry events helping me sidestep wandering hands and sloshing drinks. That's when I see him.

Chase stands in the center of his living room, holding court like some fallen angel. A bottle of Jack dangles from his fingers, and his eyes... God, his eyes. They're glassy, unfocused, nothing like the intense green gaze that's haunted my dreams for years. His shirt is unbuttoned wrong, his hair wild, and there's a smudge of something white around his nostril.

A leggy blonde hangs off his arm, whispering in his ear, but I can tell he's not really listening. He's performing, playing the role of debauched rockstar, but there's something desperate in his movements, something broken in his laugh.

His gaze finally lands on me, and for a moment, I see *my* Chase - vulnerable, brilliant, beautiful Chase. Then his eyes harden.

"Well, well, well," he slurs, stumbling in my direction. "Look who finally decided to grace us with her presence. The big shot VP herself."

I reach for him instinctively as he sways, my hands finding his waist to steady him. He's lost weight. When did that happen?

"Chase, we need to talk. Privately."

He laughs, but it's all wrong - bitter and hollow. "Oh, now you want to talk? After weeks of radio silence?"

I glance around, acutely aware of the vultures circling, phones ready to capture any drama. "Please, Chase. Not here."

Something in my voice must get through to him because he nods, leading me upstairs to his studio. The room that was once his sanctuary is in chaos. Empty bottles everywhere. Cigarette butts crushed into handwritten lyrics. His prized guitar collection gathering dust.

As soon as the door closes, he rounds on me. "What are you doing here, Eliza? Come to check up on me? Make sure I'm not tarnishing the Blackmore brand?"

"I'm here because I'm worried about you," I say softly, fighting the urge to reach out and wipe that white smudge from his nose. "We all are. You've missed every writing session, you're not returning calls..."

"Worried?" he scoffs. "That's rich. You didn't seem too worried when you were accepting that promotion, ready to leave us behind."

I flinch at the accusation. "That's not fair, Chase. I fought to keep managing the band. I never wanted to leave you."

"Leave the band, you mean," he corrects, his eyes boring into mine. "But you've been leaving me for years, haven't you? Always keeping me at arm's length, never letting me in completely."

His words hit too close to home, and I feel tears pricking at my eyes. "Chase, please. You're high, you're drunk. You're not thinking clearly."

"No," he says, suddenly eerily calm. "I'm thinking clearly for the first time in years. You've been playing with my heart, Eliza. Stringing me along. And I'm done."

The pain in his voice cuts through me, igniting something deep inside. All the carefully maintained walls, all the professional distance I've tried to keep - it crumbles in an instant.

"I love you, damnit," I burst out, the words

exploding from somewhere deep inside me.

Chase freezes, his eyes widening. "What?"

"I love you," I repeat, my voice rising with a mix of frustration and pain. "Of course I love you. How can you not see that? Every single day, in everything I do. In every fight I've fought for you, every time I've picked up the pieces, every moment I've put your needs ahead of my own. Including right now, standing here in this mess, trying to pull you back from whatever edge you're racing toward."

I run a hand through my hair, years of pent-up feelings spilling out. "Do you think any other manager would be here right now? Do you think this is in my job description? I love you so much it terrifies me, Chase. It always has."

He takes a step toward me, hope warring with disbelief on his face. "Then why-"

"Because it's impossible," I cut him off, my voice breaking. "Because loving you isn't enough. Because there's the band to think about, and the label, and our careers. Because every time we get close to crossing that line, something like this happens." I gesture around at the chaos of his studio. "And I have to be the one to pull us back, to be the responsible one, to keep us both from burning everything to the ground."

"None of that matters," he insists, moving closer. "We can figure it out. Together."

I shake my head, even as every fiber of my being screams at me to give in. "It's not that simple, and you know it. Look at what's happening already. The drugs, the drinking, these people in your house... this isn't you, Chase."

"This is who I am without you," he says, his voice raw with emotion.

"No," I say firmly, reaching out to cup his face. His skin is clammy under my palm. "Don't you dare pin all of this on me. You don't get to blame me for any of this. This is you running away. From your talent, from your responsibilities. From yourself."

He leans into my touch, his eyes closing. For a moment, we stand there in silence, the weight of everything unsaid hanging between us. The music pounds through the floor, a chaotic counterpoint to my racing heart.

Finally, Chase speaks, his voice barely above a whisper. "So where does this leave us?"

I take a deep breath, my thumb ghosting over his cheekbone. "It leaves us where we've always been. Manager and artist. Friends. But nothing more. It has to be this way, Chase. For both our sakes. Yes, I love you, but it will never work. Why can't you see that?"

He pulls away, the walls slamming back up. "Right. Professional. Got it."

"Chase..."

"You should go," he says, turning away from me. "I've got a party to get back to. Lots of networking to do." The bitterness in his voice is like acid.

I stand there for a moment, wanting to say more,

to make him understand. But as I watch him pick up a half-empty bottle, hands shaking slightly, I realize something that terrifies me: I'm losing him. Not just professionally or romantically, but completely.

As I make my way back through the party, my heart feels like lead in my chest. Every cell in my body screams at me to turn around, to go back, to save him from himself. But I can't. Not if he won't let me.

In my car, I pull out my phone with trembling fingers. I scroll through my contacts until I find Will's number. He needs to know how bad things have gotten. We need to do something before...

I can't even finish the thought.

Don't Let It End

CHASE

THE COFFEE SHOP is quiet for a weekday afternoon. Will's already at our usual corner table, two steaming mugs waiting. Some things never change - he still remembers how I take my coffee, even if these days it's accompanied by pastries instead of hair of the dog.

"You look like shit," Will says by way of greeting, but there's warmth in his smile.

"Thanks. Always good to hear from my number one fan." I slide into the seat across from him, wrapping my hands around the mug. "How are the kids?"

"Good. Maya just made junior partner at her firm," Will grins with obvious pride. "And Lucas's band is finally getting some decent gigs. Though he still refuses to admit that his old man might know a thing or two about the industry."

We share a laugh, falling into the easy rhythm that

comes with decades of friendship. But there's an undercurrent of tension - Will knows I didn't ask him here just to catch up.

"So," he says after a moment, "want to tell me what's really on your mind?"

I stare into my coffee, gathering my thoughts. "It's the ceremony. Performing *Whispered Truths*... I've never done it for an audience sober before. Not once in twenty years."

Will's expression softens with understanding. "That's what's got you tied up in knots? Not the whole Eliza situation?"

"That's part of it. It's... complicated. But this?" I run a hand through my hair. "Every time we rehearse it, I feel like I'm going to crawl out of my skin. It's different now. Rawer. Like there's nowhere to hide."

"Maybe that's not a bad thing," Will suggests. "Your voice is stronger than ever these days. Clear. Present."

"Yeah, well, being present is exactly what scares the shit out of me." I pause, searching for the right words. "That song... it was always easier to perform when I could blur the edges, you know? Take the edge off. Now I have to feel every word."

Will nods slowly. "I remember the farewell tour. After Chicago..."

"Christ," I exhale heavily. "That was a wake-up call. Or it should have been."

"You tried after that," Will reminds me. "Did the whole rehab thing."

"For about six months," I say bitterly. "Then convinced myself I could handle just one drink. One line. We both know how that turned out."

Will's quiet for a moment, studying me. "But this time's different. Five years, man. That's real."

"Yeah." I trace the rim of my mug. "My therapist wants me to write Eliza a letter. A real apology, for everything. Not just the final spiral, but all of it."

"About time," Will says bluntly. "Though I'm pretty sure she'd rather hear it in person."

I shake my head. "It's complicated."

"It's really not." Will leans forward. "Look, we all knew about you two. The stolen moments, the lingering looks, the tension you could cut with a knife. Hell, Mark and I used to have a bet going about when you'd finally get your shit together."

"Really?" I can't help but ask. "Who won?"

"Neither of us. We never thought you'd both be so damn stubborn for so long." Will sighs. "You're sober now. Really sober, not just playing at it. You've done the work. She's not your manager anymore, not really - that's just a title she keeps because she can't let go either. So, what's stopping you?"

"Fear," I admit after a long moment. "Not just of messing things up with her again. But of doing this - performing, feeling, living - without any cushion. Without anything to take the edge off. Some days I wake up and I'm not sure I know how to be Chase Avery without chemical assistance."

"You're doing it right now," Will points out. "Have been for five years."

"Yeah, but this is different. That song... it's everything I never had the courage to say to her face. And now I have to say it in front of thousands of people, stone cold sober."

Will's expression turns serious. "Maybe that's exactly why you need to do it. Show her - and yourself - that you can feel it all and still stay standing."

I let his words sink in, feeling their weight. "When did you get so wise?"

"Probably around the same time you got your head out of your ass," he grins. Then his expression softens. "The song's always been about Eliza, Chase. But maybe this time, it needs to be about you too. About who you are now, not who you were then."

As we say goodbye outside the coffee shop, I feel lighter somehow. Maybe it's having finally voiced my fears. Maybe it's Will's unwavering support. Or maybe it's just knowing that someone else understands the magnitude of what I'm facing.

I pull out my phone and open a blank document.

Dear Eliza,

I type, then pause. After a moment, I delete it and start again.

Eliza, I remember the night you saved me in Chicago...

The words start to flow, and this time, I let them come without trying to blur their edges.

November 15, 2018

Will's new house in the Hills still feels strange. Too clean, too organized. Nothing like the chaotic crash pad we shared in our twenties, with its perpetually sticky floors and walls plastered in band posters. But the view of the city is killer, I'll give him that.

I pace the length of his deck, fingers drumming an anxious rhythm against my thigh as I wait for Mark to arrive. *Band meeting.* The words leave a sour taste in my mouth, or maybe that's just the remnants of last night's binge. My hands shake slightly as I light a cigarette, and I tell myself it's just the wind.

"That's your fourth one since you got here," Will says from behind me. I turn to find him leaning against the doorframe, arms crossed. He looks tired. We all do these days.

"You counting my smokes now?" I try for levity, but it falls flat. "What are you, my mother?"

Will doesn't smile. "No, but I am counting the

empty bottles in your recycling bin. And the missed rehearsals. And the times you've shown up too wasted to play."

Something hot and defensive rises in my chest. "I've never missed a show."

"No," Will agrees quietly. "But how long until you do?"

Before I can respond, the glass door slides open and Mark steps out. His blue hair is more grey than electric these days, but he still moves with that languid grace that made him our resident heartbreaker back in the day.

"Sorry I'm late," he says, though his tone suggests he's anything but. "Traffic was a bitch."

We settle into the outdoor furniture - expensive teak that probably cost more than our first tour van. For a moment, none of us speaks. Countless years of history hangs in the air between us, heavy with things unsaid.

"So," I break the silence, aiming for casual. "What's so important it couldn't wait until rehearsal?"

Will and Mark exchange a look that makes my stomach clench.

"We think it's time," Will says finally. "To end it. Go out while we're still on top."

The words hit me like a physical blow, even though part of me has been expecting them. "You're joking, right?"

"Chase," Mark leans forward, his voice gentle in

a way that makes me want to scream. "We're pushing forty. The industry's changing. And you're..."

"I'm what?" I challenge, heat rising in my voice. "Come on, say it."

"You're killing yourself," Will cuts in bluntly. "And we're not going to stick around and watch."

I laugh, but there's no humor in it. "So that's it? Twenty years of brotherhood, and you're just gonna walk away?"

"Brotherhood?" Mark's voice cracks slightly. "Is that what you call showing up three hours late to rehearsal, high out of your mind? Missing recording sessions because you're too hungover to function? Disappearing for days with no word, while we're left wondering if this time you've finally OD'd?"

His words cut deep, mostly because I know they're true. But I can't face that right now. Can't face any of it.

"I'm fine," I insist, even as my hands shake so badly I have to clasp them together. "I've got it under control."

"Like you had it under control in Sydney?" Will asks quietly. "Or Tokyo? Or that night in Madrid when Eliza had to talk the hotel out of calling the cops?"

The mention of Eliza's name sends a fresh wave of shame through me. She's been conspicuously absent lately, sending her assistant to deal with band matters. I tell myself it's because she's busy with her VP duties, but I know better.

"One more album," I say suddenly, the idea forming as I speak. "One final tour. Go out in style, give the fans what they deserve."

Will shakes his head. "Chase..."

"No, listen," I lean forward, the desperation I'm feeling channeling into enthusiasm. "We've got the songs. That stuff I showed you last month? It's good. You know it's good. We do it right - take our time in the studio, plan a proper farewell tour. End it on our terms."

I can see them wavering. Over two decades, I've learned exactly how to play them, how to appeal to their sense of artistry and loyalty. The guilt of manipulating them like this is just one more thing I'll drink away later.

"What about you?" Mark asks. "Can you keep it together long enough to do this right?"

"Yes," I lie, meeting his eyes steadily. "I swear. No more missed sessions, no more showing up late. I'll do whatever it takes."

Another look passes between them, loaded with twenty years of friendship and worry and love.

"One condition," Will says finally. "You get clean. Really clean. No half-measures this time."

I nod quickly, already calculating how many pills I have stashed at home. "Of course. Whatever you need."

"We mean it, Chase," Mark adds. "First slip-up, first missed rehearsal because you're too fucked up to play, and we pull the plug. No arguments."

"Deal," I agree, even as part of me knows I'm making promises I can't keep. But I'll worry about that later. Right now, I just need to keep the band together, keep the music going. It's all I have left.

Will stands, running a hand through his hair - a gesture so familiar it makes my chest ache. "Alright. One last album. One last tour. Then we're done."

As we head inside to hash out the details, I catch my reflection in Will's sliding glass door. For a moment, I barely recognize myself - the shadows under my eyes, the tension in my jaw, the slight tremor in my hands that never quite goes away these days.

I look away quickly. One last album. One last tour. One last chance to prove to everyone - to Eliza, to the band, to myself - that I'm not as far gone as they think.

I can do this. I have to.

But even as I make plans with Will and Mark, part of me knows I'm lying. To them, to myself, to everyone. Because the truth is, I don't know how to make music sober anymore. Don't know how to feel anything without chemical assistance. Don't know who Chase Avery is without the buzz of alcohol in his veins or powder in his nose.

I guess we'll all find out soon enough.

New Way Out

ELIZA

I'M late to the photo shoot, having lost track of time in a budget meeting that ran long. My heels click rapidly against the polished concrete floors of the studio as I hurry to check in, muttering apologies to the coordinator who's clearly been waiting.

"They're already started," she informs me, leading the way. "Just getting some shots of the band first, then-"

I don't hear the rest of her sentence. My brain short-circuits at the sight of Chase.

His hair. God, his hair. Gone are the shaggy rock-star locks I've known for two decades, replaced by a sleek undercut that somehow makes him look both older and younger at once. The longer top is artfully tousled, and there's a neat beard shadowing his jaw, silver threads catching the studio lights. He looks...

Professional. Put together. Devastatingly handsome.

I realize I'm staring when Will catches my eye and smirks. Thankfully, everyone else is focused on the photographer's instructions.

"Alright, Chase, lean on Will's shoulder - yeah, perfect. Now Mark, if you could just..."

I busy myself with my phone, pretending to check emails while sneaking glances. The new look transforms him from aging rockstar to distinguished musician. It suits him. Suits the man he's become.

"Ms. Kerr!" The photographer's voice makes me jump. "Perfect timing. We need some shots with management."

"Oh, I don't think-" I start, but I'm already being herded toward the group.

"Here, between Chase and Will," the photographer directs, and suddenly I'm there, hyperaware of Chase's proximity, of the heat radiating from his body.

"Hey," he says softly, just for me. "You're late."

I risk a glance up at him, and my heart stutters. This close, I can see the laugh lines around his eyes, the silver in his beard. His eyes are clear, present. No haze of substances dulling that intense green.

"Budget meetings," I manage. "You look... different."

A small smile plays at his lips. "Good different?"

Before I can answer, the photographer calls for

another configuration, and we're shifting, moving. Each new pose brings a fresh point of contact - his hand at the small of my back, my shoulder brushing his chest. It's professional, necessary. So why does each touch feel like electricity?

"Actually," the photographer says, reviewing his screen, "let's get a few of just Ms. Kerr and Chase. The rest of you can take five."

My stomach drops. Will and Mark exchange knowing looks as they step away, leaving Chase and me alone in front of the lights.

"Chase, if you could..." The photographer gestures, and suddenly Chase is behind me, one hand resting lightly on my waist. Professional. Casual. Except nothing about Chase's touch has ever been casual.

"Relax," Chase murmurs, his breath warm against my ear. "You look like you're being held hostage."

I want to elbow him, but I force a smile for the camera instead. "I hate having my picture taken. You know that."

"I remember," he says softly. "London, 2008. That press junket where you made me stand in front of you in every shot."

The memory hits me with surprising force - Chase, laughing, playing human shield while I hid from the paparazzi. Things were simpler then. Or maybe we just thought they were.

"Perfect, hold that!" The photographer's voice

breaks through my reverie. "That connection - whatever you just said to her, Chase, say it again. Yes! There it is!"

I realize I've turned my head slightly, looking up at Chase, and he's looking down at me with such tenderness it makes my chest ache. For a moment, I forget about the cameras, the people watching, everything except the way he's looking at me.

Click. Click. Click.

"Beautiful," the photographer murmurs. "Absolutely beautiful. Come see."

We break apart, the spell shattered. On the photographer's screen, I watch him scroll through the shots. My breath catches.

There we are, caught in that unguarded moment. Chase's new look is striking, yes, but it's our expressions that grab me. The way we're looking at each other... there's no denying what's there. No pretending it's just professional. No hiding behind carefully constructed walls.

"This one's magic," the photographer says, obviously pleased. "You can feel the history between you."

I step back quickly, nearly stumbling. "I should check in with the stylist about the ceremony outfits," I say, my voice not quite steady. "Excuse me."

I'm halfway to the door when Chase calls after me. "Eliza."

I pause but don't turn. Can't turn. Can't look at him right now.

"For what it's worth," he says quietly, "I think the beard makes me look distinguished."

A laugh escapes me before I can stop it. Trust Chase to know exactly how to break the tension. "Distinguished might be pushing it," I say over my shoulder. "But it's not terrible."

His answering chuckle follows me out of the studio. In the hallway, I lean against the wall, taking deep breaths.

That photo. God, that photo. It's going to be everywhere - magazines, websites, the ceremony program. Evidence of everything I've tried so hard to hide, captured in perfect high-resolution.

My phone buzzes - a text from Michelle.

> MICHELLE: Saw the proofs. Girl, we
> need to talk.

That was fucking quick. I close my eyes, remembering the silver in Chase's beard, the warmth of his hand on my waist, the way he looked at me like no time had passed at all.

Distinguished, indeed.

I am in so much trouble.

November 18, 2018

The conference room feels too small for this conversation. I sit at the head of the table, my expression carefully neutral as Will finishes explaining their decision. Twenty years of practice keeps my hands steady as I make notes, even as my heart pounds painfully against my ribs.

"A farewell tour," I repeat, my voice professional, detached. "And one final album."

"We thought it was time," Will says gently. His eyes flick to Chase, who's been studying his hands since the meeting began. "Go out on our own terms, you know?"

I nod, like this is just another business decision. Like they're not telling me my world is about to end. "Of course. That's... that's very wise. We'll need to plan this carefully. Make it special for the fans."

Mark shifts in his seat. "Chase said you'd understand."

At his name, Chase finally looks up, but not at me. Never at me. "We've got the songs," he says, his voice slightly too bright. "Best stuff we've written in years."

Something's off about him. His movements are

too sharp, his smile too wide. I've spent two decades learning Chase's tells, and right now, every instinct I have is screaming that something's wrong.

"Well," I say, shuffling my papers to hide the tremor in my hands, "we should start planning immediately. I'll have my team put together some preliminary tour routes, and we'll need to book studio time-"

"Actually," Chase interrupts, still not meeting my eyes, "we were thinking of using Revolution Studios. Fresh start, new sound."

Revolution Studios. All the way across town from my office. Away from my oversight.

"I see." I make another note, my pen pressing too hard into the paper. "That could work. Though their rates are-"

"We'll handle it," Chase says quickly. "You don't need to worry about any of that."

Finally, he looks at me, and what I see in his eyes makes my blood run cold. His pupils are pinpricks, and there's a feverish sheen to his skin that I recognize all too well.

"Well," I stand, needing to end this meeting before my composure cracks completely. "Send me the demos when you have them. We'll set up a proper production schedule."

The band files out, but Chase lingers. I busy myself with my laptop, not trusting myself to look at him directly.

"Eliza," he says softly. "Can we talk?"

I should say no. Every instinct is telling me to maintain professional distance. Instead, I hear myself say, "Close the door."

He does, then leans against it, running a hand through his hair. "Are you okay?"

A laugh escapes me before I can stop it. "Am I okay? You're ending the band, Chase. After twenty years. And you couldn't even look at me while telling me."

"It's not like that," he starts, taking a step toward me. "This is... it's better this way. Ending it right, you know?"

I force myself to really look at him. His skin is waxy under the fluorescent lights, and he can't seem to stand still. "Are you clean?" I ask quietly.

"Of course," he says, too quickly. "I promised the guys, didn't I? Totally clean."

Lie. God, such an obvious lie. But he's gotten better at hiding it, or maybe I've gotten too tired to fight.

"Chase..."

"Listen," he cuts me off, moving closer. "I've been thinking. Once this is done - the album, the tour, all of it - we won't be working together anymore. No more professional complications."

My heart stutters. "What are you saying?"

"I'm saying," he reaches for my hand, and I try not to notice how his fingers tremble, "maybe we could finally stop pretending. Be together for real."

For a moment, I let myself imagine it. Chase and me, no contracts or careers between us. No more hiding, no more pretending.

But then I see the signs I've been trying to ignore - the slight shake in his hands, the too-bright eyes, the restless energy radiating off him in waves. Whatever he's on, it's not just alcohol anymore.

"Chase," I say carefully, pulling my hand away, "let's... let's focus on the album first. Make sure this farewell is everything it should be."

Something flashes in his eyes - hurt? Anger? - but it's gone so quickly I might have imagined it. "Right," he says, his voice hardening slightly. "Always the professional."

"That's not fair."

"Isn't it?" He steps back, and I feel the distance like a physical thing. "Twenty years, Eliza. Twenty years of 'not the right time' and 'too complicated.' When is it going to be simple enough for you?"

When you're really clean, I want to say. *When I'm not terrified that loving you means watching you destroy yourself.*

Instead, I say, "We should focus on the band right now. Everything else... we can figure that out later."

He laughs, but there's no warmth in it. "Later. Right. There's always later with you, isn't there?"

Before I can respond, he's gone, the door clicking shut behind him with devastating finality.

I sink into my chair, the professional mask finally

cracking. Tears burn behind my eyes, but I blink them back. Not here. Not now.

My phone buzzes - a text from Will.

> WILL: Keep an eye on him, okay?
> He's not as fine as he wants us to
> think.

I stare at the message, my vision blurring. Oh, Will. If only you knew how hard that is to do when someone's determined to destroy themselves.

My gaze falls on a framed photo on my desk - the band's first gold record celebration. We're all so young, so full of hope. Chase has his arm around my waist, both of us laughing at something off-camera.

I turn the frame face-down. I can't look at that Chase right now, can't reconcile him with the man who just left my office, vibrating with barely controlled chaos.

One last album. One last tour.

Please, I think, though I'm not sure who I'm praying to, don't let it be the end of him too.

The Road to Hell

I'VE REWRITTEN this letter at least seventeen times. The latest version sits on my desk, coffee rings staining the corners, words crossed out and rewritten until the paper's nearly transparent in spots. Dr. Hendricks says writing it is part of my recovery, even if I never give it to her. Will thinks I should focus on getting through the ceremony first. Mark just handed me his guitar yesterday and said "Write a fucking song instead."

But songs are what got us here in the first place.

My phone buzzes with another text from Will about travel arrangements for Cleveland. Two weeks. Two weeks until I have to perform *Whispered Truths* stone cold sober while she watches from the wings. Twenty years of hiding behind a chemical curtain, and now I have to lay myself bare in front of the entire industry.

A text from Michelle breaks my downward thought spiral.

> MICHELLE: Looking good in those photos, Avery. Though maybe next time try not to look at my boss like you want to devour her in front of the photographer.

I scrub a hand over my face, feeling the neat edges of my beard. The undercut was an impulse decision last month – needed something to mark five years clean that wasn't another tattoo. But the way Eliza's eyes widened when she saw it, the way her fingers twitched like she wanted to touch it...

"Focus," I mutter, pushing away from my desk. The Malibu sunrise streams through the windows, painting everything gold. Five years ago, I'd have been coming down from something right about now, not watching the dawn.

My phone buzzes again. Will.

"Yeah?" I answer, heading for the kitchen.

"You see the proofs?" His voice has that careful tone he uses when he thinks I might break.

"Not yet." I grab a smoothie from the fridge. Kale and whatever else my nutritionist swears by these days. "That bad?"

"Depends on your definition of bad." A pause. "You two look like you're about three seconds from tearing each other's clothes off in half of them."

The smoothie turns to ash in my mouth. "Fuck."

"Pretty much what everyone who's seen them is thinking, yeah." He sighs. "You need to get your head straight before Cleveland. This limbo thing isn't working for anyone."

I lean against the counter, pressing my forehead to the cool granite. "You know what the last thing I said to her was? Before that failed rehab?"

"Chase—"

"I told her she was a coward. That she'd rather hide behind her desk than admit what was between us was real." My laugh sounds hollow even to me. "Five years sober and I still haven't figured out how to apologize for that one, or the one after that. Shit there's so much..."

"Maybe that's because you weren't entirely wrong." Will's voice softens. "You just picked the worst possible way to say it. And the worst possible times."

The memory of that night threatens to surface – the chaos backstage, the pills in my pocket, the look in her eyes when security pulled me away. I push it back down where it belongs.

"The bands want to run through the arrangements one more time before Cleveland," Will says. "You gonna be okay with that?"

I stare at my hands. They're steady now. Five years steady.

"Yeah," I say, even though we both know it's more hope than certainty. "I'll be there."

I hang up and pull up the camera roll on my phone, thumb hovering over the folder marked "Hall of Fame Shoot." One click and I'll see what everyone else is talking about. See if the camera caught what I felt crackling between us every time our eyes met.

Instead, I turn back to the letter on my desk. Cross out another line. Start again.

Dear Eliza, Twenty years ago, you saved my life by believing in our music. Five years ago, you saved it again by forcing me to face myself...

My hands are shaking now, but not from withdrawal. Some addictions, it turns out, never really let you go.

August 2018

The lights are too bright. Everything's too bright. The bass line to *Burning Bridges* thrums through my bones, but I can't remember if I'm playing the right notes. Doesn't matter. Nothing matters except the rage burning under my skin and the cocktail of chemicals trying to put it out.

Someone in the front row is filming. They're all always fucking filming, aren't they? Little rectangular lights in a sea of faces. Documenting every fucking moment of our farewell tour. Every mistake. Every missed cue. Every time Eliza watches from the wings with that look in her eyes.

Is she watching now?

The guy with the phone is shouting something. I can read his lips: *fucking junkie*.

I don't remember jumping. One second I'm on stage, the next I'm throwing punches, surrounded by screaming fans. Fists connect with flesh. The phone crunches under someone's boot. Security's trying to pull me back but I'm fighting them too, everything a blur of sweat and blood and chemicals burning through my veins.

They drag me backstage. I'm screaming something about the show, about finishing the set. Will's there, saying words I can't process. Mark's shaking his head. And Eliza—

Eliza.

She stands in the hallway, still wearing that black leather jacket that makes her eyes look like storm clouds. Steel grey swimming with concern.

"Get out." Her voice cuts through the chaos.

Everyone scatters except the two security guards holding me up. "Now. Everyone out."

"Eliza." My tongue feels too thick. "Show's not over. Gotta finish. Gotta—the lights are wrong. Everything's wrong."

"Chase..." Her voice softens as she steps closer. "What did you take?"

"You're a coward," I slur, because my brain's shorting out and nothing makes sense except her face swimming in front of me. "Hide behind your desk while I'm out here... out here bleeding music. S'all wrong. The songs don't work anymore. They just... they just keep screaming and screaming and I can't make them stop and you're not... you're supposed to... why aren't you fixing it? You always fix it. Fix me. Please, 'Liza, just..."

The concern in her eyes deepens. She reaches for my face and I lean into her touch like a dying man reaching for salvation.

"Chase, baby, you're not making sense." Her thumb strokes my cheek. When did she start crying? "I need you to focus. What's in your system?"

The pills in my pocket feel like they're burning through the denim. New ones. Guy outside promised they'd keep me flying. Keep the music from screaming.

"Can't..." The room's spinning faster now. There's a roaring in my ears like distant waves. "Can't remember. Everything's too bright. You're too bright. Always so bright..."

"Chase? Chase, look at me."

I try. God, I try. But the darkness is winning and my body's not listening and—

The last thing I feel is her hands on my face. The last thing I hear is her voice breaking as she screams for someone to call 911.

Then nothing.

The hospital room comes into focus slowly. Everything hurts - sharp, raw, real pain that tells me the drugs are finally leaving my system. There's a steady beeping somewhere to my left.

And Eliza.

She's curled in a chair by my bed, still wearing that leather jacket. Her platinum hair's a mess, purple ends tangled. Mascara tracks map the path of every tear she's shed.

"How..." My throat feels like sandpaper. "How long?"

Her eyes flutter open. Steel grey meets mine, red-rimmed and exhausted but so full of love it hurts to look at directly.

"Three days." Her voice cracks. "You seized twice

in the ambulance. Once more at the hospital. They had to restart your heart."

Jesus.

"You stayed."

She reaches for my hand, careful of the IV. Her fingers tremble against mine.

"Of course I stayed." Fresh tears spill down her cheeks. "I'll always stay. But I can't... I can't keep watching you destroy yourself. It's killing me, Chase."

I try to squeeze her hand. Try to find words that will make this better. But there aren't any. Not anymore.

"I know," I whisper.

She brings our joined hands to her lips, pressing a kiss to my knuckles. "I love you. I've always loved you. But I can't do this anymore."

She stands, smoothing her wrinkled clothes with her free hand. Three days' worth of wrinkles. When she lets go of my hand, it feels like a final chord fading out.

"Get help," she whispers. "Really get help this time. Please."

I watch her walk away, my vision blurring at the edges from exhaustion and withdrawal. The sound of her heels on linoleum echoes in my head long after she's gone.

When I wake up again, she's gone. The nurses have left my personal effects in a clear plastic bag:

wallet, phone, keys... and the silver guitar pick she gave me at our ten-year anniversary party. Even high out of my mind, I'd kept it in my pocket. Always do.

I close my fingers around it, feeling the edges bite into my palm. One more chance. One more rehab. One more promise I'm not sure I can keep.

Can U See Me in the Dark?

ELIZA

I'VE DRIVEN past his Malibu house at least a dozen times in the last five years. Never stopped. Never called. Just the occasional slow drive-by, checking for signs of life. Making sure the lights were still on.

Today, I park in his driveway.

The sun's setting over the Pacific, painting everything in shades of gold and pink. Through the floor-to-ceiling windows, I can see him pacing in his living room, phone to his ear. Even from here, I recognize his "talking to Will" posture – one hand raking through his hair, messing up that undercut that's been haunting my dreams since the photo shoot.

God, those photos.

Michelle forwarded them to me this morning with a single comment: *We need to talk about this before the ceremony.*

She was right. The chemistry radiating from every shot was undeniable. Professional distance crumbling with every frame. By the final set, we might as well have been the only two people in the room.

I press the doorbell before I can talk myself out of it.

Chase opens the door mid-laugh at something Will must have said. The sound dies in his throat when he sees me.

"I'll call you back," he says into the phone, never taking his eyes off mine.

I've seen him in various states over twenty years – drunk, high, sober, everything in between. But this... this clear-eyed intensity is something new. Something real.

"The photos?" he asks, stepping back to let me in.

"The photos." I move past him, catching his scent – coffee and whatever expensive shampoo he uses now. No alcohol. No cigarettes. Nothing artificial. Just Chase. "Michelle thinks we need to talk about them before Cleveland."

"Michelle needs to mind her own business." But there's no heat in his words. He follows me into the living room, keeping a careful distance. "You want coffee? Water? I think I have some of that herbal tea you like."

"You remember my tea preference?"

"I remember everything about you, Eliza."

I pull up short at his words before carefully

turning away to hide my reaction, trying to regain my composure.

He must see something in my expression because he backs off, heading for the kitchen. "Tea it is."

While he's gone, I study his space. Guitar collection on the wall. Piano by the windows. Writing desk covered in scattered papers. One sheet catches my eye – handwritten, coffee-stained, crossed out words everywhere.

"Here," he says behind me, and I turn too quickly, guilty at almost snooping. He hands me a mug – the same one I used to drink from when I'd visit during writing sessions. Another thing he's kept.

"How are you?" I ask, really looking at him. "Really?"

His hand goes to the back of his neck – a tell I've known for two decades. "Shouldn't I be asking you that? You're the one who drove out here."

"Chase."

He sighs, sinking onto the couch. After a moment's hesitation, I join him, leaving enough space between us for our history.

"I'm okay," he says finally. "Nervous about Cleveland. Terrified of performing *Whispered Truths* sober. But okay." His eyes find mine. "The photos scared the hell out of me."

"Why?"

"Because nothing's changed." His voice drops.

"Twenty years, multiple rehabs, five years clean... and one look from you still stops my heart."

My fingers tighten around the mug. "Chase—"

"Wait." He stands abruptly, goes to his desk. Comes back with the paper I'd noticed earlier. "I've been trying to write this for weeks. It's not... it's not perfect. But maybe it's time you read it."

His hands shake slightly as he holds it out. The same hands that used to shake from withdrawal now trembling for an entirely different reason.

"What is it?"

"Everything I couldn't say before... Everything I should have said after. Everything I'm still trying to say now."

I set down my mug and take the letter. His hand-writing is steadier than it used to be. No more chaotic scrawl of addiction.

Dear Eliza, Twenty years ago, you saved my life by believing in our music. Five years ago, you saved it again by forcing me to face myself...

"Read it," he says softly. "Please. Even if it changes nothing. Even if you walk out that door and we go back to professional distance until Cleveland. Just... read it."

The paper trembles in my hands. The sun's almost

gone now, painting the room in shades of blue and grey. Somewhere in the distance, waves crash against the shore.

I start to read.

September 2018

The security alert comes through during a label meeting. My phone buzzes with multiple notifications: motion detected, impact at entrance, unknown vehicle.

Then I see the video feed.

"I need to go," I say, already standing. Michelle catches my eye across the conference table – she's seen my face change. "Family emergency."

I'm halfway to my car when Justin calls.

"Mom?" His voice is tight. "There's a Porsche wrapped around the brick planter. Chase is passed out on the lawn."

Jesus Christ. It's 11:47 AM.

"Is he—"

"Breathing. Seems okay, but he's a mess. What do you want me to do?"

Five weeks. He managed five weeks in Ojai before either walking out or getting kicked out – no one seems to know which. Five weeks after Chicago.

After watching him seize in that ambulance. After sitting by his hospital bed for three days.

"Get him inside before someone calls the cops. I'm twenty minutes out."

"Mom—"

"Please, Justin. Just... keep him there. I'm coming."

I break every speed limit between Blackmore Records and home. My hands don't shake on the steering wheel. They should, but they don't. Fifteen years of crisis management with Chase has taught me how to function through the fear.

The Porsche is silver. Brand new. The passenger side is crumpled against the brick surround of my favorite maple tree. Glass glitters on the driveway like fallen stars.

I hear the shouting before I even get inside.

"—your mother's not your fucking responsibility!" Chase's voice, slurred but angry.

"No, but apparently you are!" Justin shouts back. "Always have been, right? Ever since I was eight years old, watching her piece you back together—"

I push through the front door. They're in the living room – Justin standing between Chase and the door, Chase swaying on his feet, looking like hell warmed over. His clothes are wrinkled, hair wild, eyes bloodshot.

"Justin," I say quietly. "Give us a minute."

"Mom—"

"Please."

He hesitates, then nods. Squeezes my shoulder as he passes. The front door closes behind him with a soft click.

Chase laughs. The sound is all broken glass. "Sent your guard dog away?"

"What are you doing here?"

"Ojai was bullshit." He runs a hand through his hair, leaving it standing even more on end. "All that... that mindfulness crap. Journaling. Group therapy. Couldn't think straight. Couldn't write. Couldn't—" He stumbles, catches himself on the back of the couch. "Couldn't breathe."

"So you thought driving drunk to my house at noon was the answer?"

"Needed to see you." His eyes find mine, glazed but desperate. "You didn't visit. Not once."

"Because you needed to focus on getting better. Plus, you took me off the fucking visitors list! You promised me, Chase. You promised the whole band you'd stay clean for the farewell tour. Then Chicago happened. You nearly died in that ambulance. Three days I sat in that hospital, watching you breathe, and the minute you got out, you checked yourself into Ojai. I thought... I really thought this time..."

"Better?" Another laugh, sharper this time. "*This* is better. This is... this is clarity. This is seeing everything exactly how it is. You and your... your perfect house and your perfect son and your perfect fucking life—"

"Stop it."

"Why? Because it hurts? Because you can't fix this with your corporate credit card and your industry connections?"

"Because this isn't you!" My voice cracks. "This isn't the man who promised me he was ready to get clean. This isn't the man I sat with in that hospital. This isn't—" I break off, really looking at him. His hands are shaking. His skin's ashen under the alcohol flush. "When's the last time you ate anything?"

The question seems to throw him. "What?"

"Food, Chase. When did you last eat?"

He sways again, frowning like he's trying to remember. "Yesterday? Maybe?"

"Sit down before you fall down. I'm making coffee."

"'Eliza—"

"Sit. Down."

He collapses onto the couch while I head for the kitchen. I can feel him watching me as I move around the space, muscle memory taking over – coffee, mugs, the bread I know he can keep down even hungover. My hands are amazingly steady as I work, even though I want to jump out of my skin.

When I come back, he's got his head in his hands.

"Here." I set coffee and toast in front of him. "Small sips."

He looks up at me, and for the first time today, I see clarity fighting through the haze. "Why are you doing this?"

"Because I love you." The words come easily, even now. Especially now. "Because I've loved you for fifteen years, through every disaster and every triumph. And because I need you to really hear me right now."

I sit beside him, not touching, but close enough to catch him if he falls.

"Do you know what it was like?" My voice is quiet. "Watching you spiral through that tour? Every night, wondering if this would be the one where you finally went too far? Then Chicago happened, and I... I had to watch you die, Chase. Three times in that ambulance. Do you have any idea what that did to me?"

He stares into his coffee. "I'm sorry."

"I know you are. But sorry isn't enough anymore. When you checked into Ojai, I thought... I let myself hope. Five weeks, Chase. Five weeks of thinking maybe this time it would stick. And now you're here, drunk at noon, wrapped around my tree."

"I couldn't..." He takes a shaky sip of coffee. "I couldn't stop thinking about you. About us. About everything we've never—"

"Stop." I take the mug from his trembling hands, set it down. "We made that 'no strings' rule for a reason, Chase. And I've never lied to you about how I feel. Never pretended I didn't love you. But I've also been clear about why we couldn't be more. The band, the label, our careers... they were too intertwined. One wrong move and it all would have collapsed."

He starts to protest but I press on. "I've respected your life choices. Never interfered with your relationships, your decisions. I didn't say a word about that Vegas wedding, or any of the girlfriends, or the partying. When other labels started circling after your third album went platinum, I supported you exploring your options. I've loved you enough to let you live your own life, to keep our professional relationship solid. Do you know how many board meetings I've sat through defending you? How many times I've put my reputation on the line to protect you from your own mistakes?"

I run a hand through my hair, dislodging pins. "Remember the Grammy incident? When you kissed me on the way to the stage? I'm the one who spun it to the press as a theatrical moment. I'm the one who convinced the board it was good publicity. Every time you've pushed those boundaries, I've been there to maintain them. Because that was our agreement. Because it was the only way this could work."

His hands are shaking worse now. "I never asked you to protect me."

"No, you just expected it. And I did it, because I believed in your talent. In the band. In you." I gesture at him, at the wreckage outside. "But this? This isn't about us. This isn't about some great star-crossed love story. This is about you using the idea of us as an excuse. You're trying to make me responsible for your choices, and I won't do it anymore."

He stares into his coffee like it holds answers. "The tour... I really thought I could stay clean. For you. For us."

"That's exactly the problem. It was never supposed to be for me, Chase. You can't hang your sobriety on someone else. Not me, not the band, not some perfect future you've imagined." I take a breath, soften my voice. "Listen to me. *Really* listen. There can't be an us until you're healthy. Not because I don't love you. Not because I don't want it. But because I cannot watch you die again. I won't survive it this time."

He snickers sarcastically. "Oh, is that the new excuse now?"

"What?"

He glares at me sideways, his mood shifting dark yet again. "There's always an excuse, isn't there? Some made up fucking reason about why we'd never work. The carrot at the end of the stick dangling right in front of my fucking face. Do you fucking get off on it or something?"

I stiffen at the change in him. "You know damn well that's not what this is."

"Do I?" he snorts, putting his coffee mug down to face me. When our eyes meet, I see a hatred there that

I've never seen him direct at me before, and I feel myself shrink back. "I don't know fucking shit when it comes to you. I never fucking have. And you... you're a god damned coward. Using every excuse in the book, and even making up more as you go to push me away. Well, I'm fucking gone now, Eliza, okay? You did it! You win! I fucking hate you. How's that?"

I'm stunned as he jolts up from the couch and starts pacing again. His words cutting deeper than anything could. I don't know if it's the alcohol talking, or if he means it. Don't people tell the truth when they're drunk? I don't know what's happening now.

"Maybe I should have died in that ambulance," he mutters, trying to pace but staggering.

"Don't say that," I jump up to steady him but he waves me off, and pushes me away.

"Don't touch me," he warns angrily. "You don't get to fucking touch me anymore. Never again you fucking coward." He leans over the back of the couch unsteadily pointing a finger at me. "You fucking did this to me, you selfish bitch."

I lean back as if he's slapped me, and I'm flooded with guilt. Is what he's saying right? Did I do this to him? Drive him to this madness? Could I really be the reason for his downward spiral?

Tears spring from my eyes unbidden as I feel the sheer hatred directed at me – where it belongs. I did do this, didn't I? This is all my fault.

"Chase, I..." My words of admission and regret

don't come fast enough as he rounds the couch and pulls me into a hug. The emotional whiplash is over-whelming.

"I'm sorry. I'm so fucking sorry, Eliza. I didn't mean that. I didn't mean any of that, I swear." He rocks me back and forth, and I can't seem to make head or tails of what's happening. "I don't know what I'm saying anymore. I don't know what I'm doing. I'm so fucking confused all the time...I just...I swear I didn't mean that."

I rub his back, trying to piece together what's real and what isn't. What's true and what's not. But I can't shake the hurt his angry words caused that is still reverberating in my bones. I think that's going to be permanent.

Hating to let him go, I pull away slowly, trying to gather myself again into the strong friend I'm supposed to be right now. Not the broken woman with guilt the size of Mount Rushmore, and pain deeper than the ocean.

The silence stretches between us, broken only by the tick of the kitchen clock. Finally, he looks at me, really looks at me, and I see the man I love fighting his way through the chaos.

"I'm scared," he whispers.

"I know." I take his hand, feel it shaking in mine. "But you're stronger than this. You're stronger than the drugs and the drinking and all the ways you try to numb yourself. I've seen that strength. I believe in it. I need you to believe in it too."

He squeezes my hand, and for a moment, I let myself remember every other time we've sat like this, on the edge of change that never quite happened.

"What do I do?" he asks, voice small.

"You get real help. Not five weeks. Not surface-level rehab. Real, deep, hard work on yourself. And this time..." I take a breath. "This time, I can't be your reason. You have to do it for you."

The sun's moved across the sky while we've been talking. The broken glass in the driveway throws rainbow prisms on the walls.

"I'm tired," he says finally, voice cracking. "I'm so fucking tired, Eliza."

Something breaks in my chest. Maybe in both of us. Because suddenly he's crying – real tears, not the drunk, maudlin kind. The kind he's probably been holding back for years.

"Come here," I whisper, and he folds into my arms like a collapsing star.

We sit there, tangled together on my couch, both of us breaking apart. His body shakes against mine as years of damage pours out of him. I hold him through it, my own tears falling into his hair, one hand curved around the back of his neck like I used to do when he was strong and brilliant and not yet scarred by all of this.

"I don't know how to do this," he mumbles against

my shoulder. "I don't know how to be clean and still be me."

"You are not your addiction." I press my lips to his temple. "The man I love – the real Chase – he's still in there. The one who wrote *Off the Record* in one night because the melody wouldn't let him sleep. The one who spent three hours teaching Justin power chords when he was nine. The one who sees music in everything. That's who you are."

He pulls back just enough to look at me, eyes red but clearer than they've been all day. "Help me?" The words are barely a whisper. "Please? Not... not like before. But help me find somewhere I actually want to go? Somewhere that might work?"

"Of course." I brush his hair back from his face, the gesture as natural as breathing. "We'll research facilities together. Find one that feels right to you. And when you're ready – really ready – I'll take you there myself."

"You'd do that? After everything?"

"Oh, baby." I rest my forehead against his. "I'd walk through fire for you. I always have. I just can't walk through it for you anymore."

He nods, understanding finally reaching through the haze. The emotional toll of the day crashes over us both, and I feel him growing heavier against me. I should move us to separate rooms. Should maintain those careful boundaries we've drawn in the sand.

Instead, I let him sink deeper into my embrace as

we both slide into exhaustion. His breathing steadies against my collar bone. My fingers card through his hair on autopilot. The afternoon sun paints warm stripes across us through the windows.

Just before sleep takes me, I feel him mumble against my neck, "Will you help me make some calls tomorrow? When I'm sober?"

"Yes," I whisper into his hair, knowing this isn't the end of his struggle. That there's still more darkness to come before he finds his way out. But for now, for this moment, he's safe in my arms. We both are.

I drift off to the steady rhythm of his heartbeat, proof that he's still alive, still here, still fighting.

It has to be enough.

Justin finds us hours later, when the sun has shifted to early evening. He doesn't wake us. Just drapes a blanket over us both and quietly cleans up the broken glass in the driveway.

Some things don't need words.

Better Days

ELIZA

Dear Eliza,

Twenty years ago, you saved my life by believing in our music. Five years ago, you saved it again by forcing me to face myself and driving me to rehab yourself, even after everything I'd said and done.

MY HANDS TREMBLE as I read, the paper catching the last rays of sunset through Chase's windows. He's hovering in the doorway, silent, watching.

I've written this letter twenty-three times. Each version tries to explain, to apologize, to make sense of what I did to us. But the truth is simple: I was the coward. Not just during the addiction, but after. Especially after.

Do you remember that afternoon we fell asleep on your couch? After I crashed into your tree? After I spewed a shit ton of venom at you that wasn't true, you held me while I cried, and for the first time in years, I felt safe. Ready to get help. Ready to change. And the next morning, you helped me find a place, and packed a bag for me. Even drove me to the facility yourself. Stayed until I was checked in.

I close my eyes, remembering. The long drive. The way his hand shook in mine as we pulled up to the gates. The last look we shared before the doors closed between us.

I'd like to say I blocked your number because I was focusing on recovery. That I was following the counselors' advice about cutting ties. But that's another lie to add to my collection. I blocked you because I was ashamed. Because the man you believed in had turned into someone who drove drunk *into your tree at noon. Someone who'd nearly died in Chicago. Someone who'd blamed you for his own destruction.*

Then COVID hit, and isolation made it easy to convince myself that silence was better. That you were better off without me in your life at all. I told myself I was giving you peace. Really, I was protecting myself from facing what I'd done.

The words blur. I blink hard, refusing to let the tears fall.

Will kept me updated about you. Told me about your promotion to President. About Justin's band. I read every industry article that mentioned you. Watched every interview. Convinced myself that keeping this distance was my last gift to you. That I'd burned too many bridges. Caused too much pain.

You spent fifteen years watching me try to kill myself. Fifteen years cleaning up my messes. Protecting me. Believing in me. Loving me despite everything. And how did I repay that love? By disappearing. By watching your life from a safe distance, too cowardly to even tell you I was finally the man you always believed I could be.

Chase shifts in the doorway. I can feel his eyes on me, but I keep reading.

The truth? You were the bravest person in my story. You loved me enough to drive me to those gates. To let me go. To say 'enough.'

I'd like to say getting clean was about you. That I did it to win you back. But that would be another lie. I got clean because you were right — I had to do it for me. Had to find out who Chase was without the drugs. Without the drama. Without using you as a safety net.

Five years sober, and I'm finally facing some hard truths:

I hid behind our 'no strings' rule because commitment terrified me more than addiction.

I used our history as an excuse to avoid dealing with my present.

I hurt you. Repeatedly. Deliberately. Unforgivably.

And even after getting clean, I was too much of a coward to face you.

So I'm saying it now: I'm sorry, Eliza. For the rehabs that didn't stick. For Chicago. For your tree. For every time I made you choose between loving me and saving yourself. For five years of silence when you deserved so much more.

The tears fall freely now, dropping onto the paper. The ink smears under them.

I convinced myself we were over. That too much pain lived in our history. I watched you build your empire from afar and told myself it was better this way. Safer. Cleaner.

Then I saw you at that photo shoot, and every lie I'd told myself about being over you shattered in an instant.

I'm not asking for another chance. I haven't earned that. But I need you to know that the man you see now — the one who's been clean for five years, who can finally look himself in the mirror — he exists because you were strong enough to take me to those gates. To let me walk through them alone.

You once told me I was stronger than my addiction. You believed that even when I didn't. Even when I couldn't. Thank you for that belief. For every time you held me together. For every time you let me fall. For that final drive that saved my life.

I love you. I've loved you for twenty years. But for the first time, I love you without needing you to save me.

Always, Chase

The paper slips from my fingers, landing silently on the hardwood floor. Chase hasn't moved from the doorway, giving me space I'm not sure I want anymore.

"Eliza?" His voice is barely a whisper.

I turn to look at him. Really look at him. The silver threading his beard. The clear green eyes. The steady hands that haven't shaken in five years.

"You read my interviews?"

A small smile tugs at his mouth. "Every one. Will says it was masochistic."

"You could have called. After the first year. After COVID. Any time."

"I know." He takes a careful step forward. "I thought... I really thought I'd lost the right to be in your life. That staying away was the only gift I had left to give you."

I stand, my legs steadier than they should be. "Twenty-three versions?"

He nods.

"And in every single one, you thought I needed your apology?"

"I—what?"

I close the distance between us, stopping just short of touching. "I never needed you to apologize, Chase. I needed you to live. That's all I've ever needed."

Understanding dawns in his eyes, followed quickly by something that looks a lot like hope.

The sun sets behind the Pacific, painting us both in shades of gold and shadow. Twenty years of history pulse in the space between us.

His hands don't shake when he reaches for mine.

Neither do mine when I let him.

The Past Five Years

The first year after I dropped Chase at rehab, I

threw myself into work. Fourteen-hour days, back-to-back meetings, endless contract negotiations. When COVID hit, I was already operating at full throttle.

But this? This was where I excelled. While other labels floundered, I created virtual concert platforms, innovative streaming solutions, remote recording setups. Built a pandemic survival strategy that became industry standard. The board noticed.

The promotion to President came faster than anyone expected. November 2020, in the middle of another COVID surge. The PR photos show me in my signature look – platinum hair with purple ends, steel grey power suit that matched my eyes. The industry papers called it a "meteoric rise."

They didn't see me almost call Chase that night. Almost text: *I did it. I finally did it.*

I deleted his number instead. Again.

"You need to date," Michelle insisted, eighteen months into my self-imposed isolation. "I know this great guy—"

"I'm fine."

But she persisted. So did Justin. So, I went on the dates. The investment banker who talked about his portfolio all through dinner. The producer who spent the whole night pitching his "innovative new sound" (it wasn't). The session musician who looked nothing like Chase but played bass, and that was enough to end that experiment.

"Mom." Justin sprawled across my office couch,

fresh from his own band's rehearsal. "When's the last time you did something just for you?"

"I just signed three new artists."

"That's work."

"I bought new shoes."

"To wear to work."

I did know what he meant. But I also knew that I had everything I needed. Great friends. A talented son whose band was making waves in the indie scene (without any help from his mother, thank you very much). A career I'd built through talent and hard work. The respect of an entire industry.

So what if I still changed radio stations when *Off the Record* came on? So what if I took the long way around the building to avoid the recording studio where...

I was fine.

Really.

"There's this guy in A&R," Michelle tried again in 2022. "Really nice. Totally your type."

"I don't have a type."

She gave me a look. "Tall. Musical. Green eyes—"

"Meeting," I said, standing abruptly. "Very important meeting."

"It's seven PM."

"Did I mention it's important?"

I dated the A&R guy briefly. And a talent scout.

And a music journalist who at least made me laugh. None of them lasted more than a few months. One took me to a restaurant where Incendiary Ink's first platinum record hung on the wall. I left before the appetizers.

"Maybe I'm just not built for relationships," I told Michelle over wine one night. "Maybe this is enough."

She didn't argue. Just topped off my glass and changed the subject to quarterly projections.

The industry papers called me an ice queen. Married to my work. Unavailable.

They weren't wrong.

I kept tabs on Chase as much as I could through Will, though I pretended not to. Clean. Sober. Living quietly in Malibu. Writing songs I pretended not to wonder about.

"He asks about you," Will mentioned casually in 2023. "Never directly. But he does."

I changed the subject. Ignored how my heart clenched.

The days blurred together in a pleasant haze of success. Board meetings. Contract signings. Industry events where I sparkled and charmed and never let anyone too close. My life looked perfect on paper.

I threw myself into Justin's career instead of my personal life. Attended his shows when I could, but always checked the venue first. Some places held too many memories. The Viper Room. The studio at

Blackmore. That little jazz club where Chase first played me *Burning Bridges* at 3 AM.

"You should come to our show Friday," Justin said one night. "We're covering some classic rock."

"Any particular classic rock?"

His silence was answer enough.

The invitations kept coming. Music industry mixers. Label parties. Award shows. I attended them all, perfectly coiffed, perfectly professional. The rare times I ran into Will or Mark, we exchanged pleasant small talk. Pretended not to notice the empty space between us where someone else should be.

"Did you hear?" Michelle asked carefully one morning. "Chase is five years sober."

"That's wonderful," I said, and meant it. "Meeting in five?"

"It's seven AM."

"Did I mention it's important?"

My life was good. Was enough.

Really.

Some lies we tell ourselves because the truth is too loud to hear.

Even when it's played through stadium speakers.

Even when it's written in platinum records on our office walls.

Even when it's echoed in every bass line on the radio.

Alive Again

CHASE

HER HAND FITS in mine exactly the same way it did twenty years ago. Some things, it seems, muscle memory never forgets.

"We were idiots," she says softly, thumb tracing patterns on my palm. "Thinking we could compartmentalize this. Draw neat little lines between personal and professional."

"The 'no strings' rule." I laugh, but there's no bitterness now. Just understanding. "Probably the biggest lie we ever told ourselves."

"We thought we were being smart. Well, I did." She looks up at me, steel grey eyes catching the last light of sunset. "Protecting the band. The label. Our careers."

"Instead we just made everything harder." I reach up, tuck a strand of platinum hair behind her ear. Her breath catches. "Every meeting. Every recording session. Every time I had to watch you leave."

"You think I didn't feel it too?" Her free hand comes up to rest against my chest, right over my heart. "Sitting in board meetings, defending your talent while trying not to let them see how much I loved you? Having to maintain professional distance when all I wanted..."

She trails off, but I feel the weight of twenty years in that unfinished sentence.

"We were trying to have it both ways," I say. "Keep the professional boundaries while pretending what was between us wasn't real. wasn't consuming us both."

"It nearly destroyed us."

"*I* nearly destroyed us." I correct her gently. "The drugs, the drinking... that was all me. You were just trying to keep everything from falling apart."

"I enabled you." Her fingers curl against my chest. "Every time I cleaned up your messes. Every time I chose the label's interests over your health. I told myself I was being professional, but really, I was just scared. Scared of losing you completely."

"Eliza..." I bring our joined hands to my lips, kiss her knuckles. "You saved my life. Multiple times."

"And nearly lost myself in the process." A tear slips down her cheek. I catch it with my thumb. "Do you know what scared me most? Not the drugs. Not the drinking. It was watching you spiral and knowing that if I chose you – really chose you – everything we'd built would collapse. The band. Your career. Mine."

"And now?"

She looks up at me, really looks at me, like she's seeing twenty years of history and possibility all at once.

"Now you've been sober five years without my help. Built your own recovery. Found yourself." Her hand slides up to cup my jaw, thumb brushing my beard. "Now I'm not watching you die anymore. I'm watching you live."

Something breaks open in my chest. "I miss you. God, Eliza, I miss you every day. Not just... not just the physical. I miss your mind. Your heart. The way you see through everyone's bullshit, especially mine. I miss my best friend."

"I'm right here." Her voice breaks. "I've always been right here."

When I kiss her, it feels like coming home. Like every song I've ever written. Like twenty years of longing distilled into a single moment.

She melts into me, both hands sliding into my hair, and suddenly we're not President and rockstar, not professional colleagues maintaining boundaries with stupid rules. We're just Chase and Eliza, finally, *finally* getting it right.

"Stay," I whisper against her lips. "Please. We've wasted so much time."

"Are you sure?" She pulls back just enough to meet my eyes. "This changes everything."

I rest my forehead against hers. "Maybe everything needs to change."

Her answer is another kiss, deeper this time. Twenty years of restraint crumbling like sand castles in the tide.

The sun sets behind us as we stumble toward my bedroom, leaving our carefully constructed boundaries scattered like paper on the floor behind us.

Some strings, it turns out, were meant to be tied all along.

More

ELIZA

TWENTY YEARS of wanting crystallizes in the press of his lips against my neck, the slide of his hands under my silk blouse. Some memories live in muscle memory – the spot behind his ear that makes him gasp, the way his hands tremble when I trace his spine. Only now, the trembling isn't from withdrawal or chemicals. It's pure want, pure presence.

"Eliza," he breathes against my collar bone, and it's a prayer, a plea, a promise all at once. "God, I've missed you. Every part of you."

Moonlight spills through his bedroom windows, painting silver streaks in his beard, catching the green of his eyes as he draws back to look at me. His fingers trace my face like he's memorizing it all over again. They're steadier now than they've ever been, certain in their path.

"You're so beautiful." His voice breaks. "You've

always been so beautiful. That night in the studio, remember? When you walked in wearing that black dress..."

"The one you wrote *Off the Record* about?" I smile against his lips. "How could I forget?"

I remember him at twenty-five, all swagger and charm, pressing me against the soundboard after everyone left. At thirty-five, desperate and burning. But this... this man who touches me with reverent hands, who looks at me like I'm everything he's ever written songs about... this is new. This is real.

My blouse falls away under his careful touch. His shirt follows. When skin meets skin, we both gasp at the contact. Different bodies now – softer curves, silver threads in hair, scars we've earned apart – but the way we fit together hasn't changed. I trace the new tattoo on his ribs, five years clean marked in elegant script. His fingers find the cesarean scar from Justin that he once kissed in a hotel room in Paris.

"I wrote about this," he murmurs, trailing kisses down my neck to that spot that makes me arch – the one he mentioned in verse two of *Burning Bridges*. "Every freckle. Every sigh. You're in every song I've ever written."

"Chase—" My voice catches as his mouth finds that sensitive place behind my knee that he somehow still remembers, the one he used to tease during meetings just to watch me try to maintain composure. "Please."

He takes his time, relearning me with lips and hands, finding old sensitive spots and discovering new ones. I remember how to make him groan – that spot on his hip, the way he loves having his hair pulled. When he finally moves above me, the weight of him familiar and new all at once, tears slip from my eyes.

"Hey." He catches them with his thumbs, his own eyes bright with emotion. "You okay?"

"Better than okay." I pull him down to me, kiss him deep and slow. "Just... overwhelmed. It's been so long. And you're so present. So here. No substances, no barriers..."

"Just us," he whispers. "Finally just us." His forehead presses to mine. "I'm done wasting time. No more hiding in addiction. No more professional distance. No more pretending you're not the love of my life."

When we move together, it's with twenty years of knowledge and fresh discovery. He still arches the same way when I drag my nails down his back. I still gasp his name the same way when he hits just the right spot, the sound he once said was better than any melody he'd ever written. But there's something different now – a depth, an understanding, a certainty we never had before.

"Look at me," he whispers as we near the edge. "Please, baby, look at me. I want to really see you this time. No haze, no blur, just you."

I do. Green eyes lock with grey, and everything we've never said passes between us. Every missed chance. Every almost. Every finally. Every lyric he wrote about this exact shade of grey.

We fall together, his name on my lips, mine on his, moonlight turning us both to silver. No rushing apart this time. No hurried redressing for emergency meetings. No walk of shame. No regrets.

After, he gathers me close, pressing soft kisses to my hair, my temples, my shoulder. His hand finds mine, fingers intertwining like they did that first night in the studio when *Off the Record* was just beginning to form in his mind.

"I love you," he murmurs against my skin. "Twenty years, and that's never changed. Not in rehab, not in success, not in failure. You're in every song because you're in every heartbeat."

I trace the familiar lines of his face, the new ones earned in sobriety, memorizing him all over again. "I love you too. Through everything. Every up, every down. Always have."

He catches my hand, kisses my palm like he used to do before every show. "Stay?"

The question holds twenty years of weight. Of times I couldn't stay. Wouldn't stay. Had to walk away. Of early morning meetings and industry appearances. Of maintaining professional distance.

"Yes," I whisper, and feel him smile against my fingers. "I'm done walking away."

The moon crosses the sky as we drift off tangled together, his heartbeat steady under my palm. Some strings, once tied, can never really break.

They just wait to be acknowledged.

"Eliza?" His voice is soft with approaching sleep.

"Hmm?"

"That black dress? I still have the zipper that broke that night in the studio. Kept it all these years."

I laugh against his chest, the sound pure joy. "Of course you did."

Some memories are meant to be kept forever.

Black Butterfly

CHASE

THE LIGHTS ARE TOO BRIGHT. They've always been too bright at these things. But for the first time in twenty years, I'm facing them sober. No pills to dull the edge. No whiskey to smooth the way. Just me, Will, and Mark at the conference table, fielding questions about the Hall of Fame ceremony.

My fingers find the silver guitar pick in my pocket – a habit so ingrained I barely notice anymore. For years I've carried it. Through hell and back. Through losing everything, including her.

Eliza stands at the back of the room with Michelle, both of them in their usual power suits. Every time I look at her, I remember last night. This morning. The way she smiled when she borrowed one of my t-shirts for breakfast.

Focus, Avery.

"Chase." A reporter in the front row – *Rolling*

Stone, I think. "How does it feel preparing to perform *Whispered Truths* sober for the first time? Especially given the... personal nature of the lyrics?"

My fingers curl around the pick. Steady. Present. "Terrifying." The honesty gets a laugh. "But right. That song deserves to be performed with clear eyes. It always has."

"Speaking of that song," another reporter jumps in. "You've never officially confirmed who it's about, but the Grammy performance in 2015—"

"The one where I kissed Eliza on the way to the stage?" I can't help smiling at the memory. "Yeah, I guess that wasn't exactly subtle."

Soft laughter ripples through the room. Eliza maintains her professional mask, but I see the slight color in her cheeks. She remembers too.

The questions continue – about the ceremony, about the bands joining us, about our legacy. Mark fields questions about our early days, Will handles the technical aspects of the performance. It's almost like old times, except I'm actually present for it. No haze, no blur, no chemical buffer between me and reality.

"And what about *Burning Bridges*?" A music blogger this time. "The whole third album seemed to chart the progression of a complicated relationship. One that coincided with Blackmore Records taking a chance on an unknown band..."

I grip the pick tighter, its edges biting into my palm.

"Those songs speak for themselves," Will interjects smoothly, following the PR script we'd prepared. But before he can continue—

"These photos were leaked online this morning."

The screen behind us flickers to life. Suddenly we're all staring at images from the photo shoot. Me and Eliza, caught in moments we didn't realize revealed everything between us. The way she looked at me. The way I couldn't look away from her. Chemistry radiating from every frame.

My heart stops. We haven't talked about going public. Haven't discussed what this means for her position at the label, for the band's legacy, for any of it. Five days of bliss in our private bubble, and now...

"The rumors about your relationship with Eliza Kerr have circulated for years." The reporter leans forward. "The industry whispers, the songs clearly about her, the infamous Grammy kiss. Care to comment on these photos? On your current relationship status? And how does this affect the professional dynamics at play?"

The room goes silent. I can feel every eye on me. Will's hand finds my shoulder – steady support, like always. Mark gives me the smallest nod.

Don't look. Don't look. Don't—

I look.

She's standing perfectly still, face unreadable behind her professional mask. The one she perfected over twenty years of keeping our secrets.

I pull out the silver guitar pick, hold it up to catch the light. Her eyes widen – she probably thought I'd lost it years ago. Lost it like I'd lost myself.

"See this?" My voice is steady. "Eliza gave me this at our ten-year anniversary party. A private moment during a public celebration. I've carried it every day since. Through addiction. Through recovery. Through five years of silence when I was too ashamed to face her."

The pick gleams under the lights as I turn it, showing the worn edges, the barely visible engraving.

"Those rumors have always been complicated by our professional relationship. By my addiction. By timing and circumstance and my own demons."

I watch her hand press against her stomach, that tell I've known for twenty years.

"The truth is, I've loved Eliza Kerr for twenty years." The words feel like freedom. Like finally singing the right note after years of being sharp. "Through every up and down. Through addiction and recovery. Through her rise to President and my fall to rock bottom. She saved my life more times than I can count, and then saved it one final time by being brave enough to give me space until I got clean."

Will squeezes my shoulder. Mark coughs to hide what might be a laugh or a sob.

"Every song – yes, including *Whispered Truths* – every Grammy performance, every moment of our success is tied to her. Not just because she believed in our music, but because she believed in me when I couldn't believe in myself. She maintained professional boundaries when I kept trying to blur them. She put her career on the line multiple times to protect me from myself."

The room erupts with questions. Cameras flash. I ignore them all, finding her eyes again across the space.

She's smiling, tears threatening to ruin her perfect makeup.

"And now?" The same reporter, voice cutting through the chaos. "What's your relationship status now? What about the conflict of interest?"

I don't look away from Eliza as I answer. "Now I think I might finally be worthy of her. Now I'm finally the man she always believed I could be. As for the professional concerns..." I smile, closing my fingers around her gift. "I think twenty years of maintaining boundaries proves we can handle it."

Her smile widens. Michelle elbows her, whispering something that makes Eliza actually laugh out loud – a sound so rare in professional settings that several heads turn.

"Jesus," Will mutters beside me, but he's smiling too. "Guess we're doing this."

"Guess we are."

The rest of the conference passes in a blur. I answer questions on autopilot, professional enough to stay on topic, but my eyes keep finding her. The way she's relaxed now, mask dropped. The way she keeps touching the collar of her blazer – where a mark from my mouth this morning hides just underneath.

When it's over, when the reporters file out and the cameras power down, she crosses the room to me. Everyone pretends not to watch.

"So," she says softly. "Worthy of me, huh?"

"Too much?" My hands itch to touch her, but we're still in public. Still navigating this new reality.

"No." She straightens my collar, fingers lingering. "Just right. Like everything else lately."

"Even though I didn't ask first? About going public?"

"Chase." Her smile is soft, private. Just for me. "You just told the world you love me. In front of cameras. Completely sober. That's... that's everything I never let myself hope for."

"I do love you." The words still feel like freedom. "Figured it was time everyone knew."

"Good." She steps back, professional mask sliding back into place, but her eyes are dancing. "Because Page Six is going to have a field day with this, and I'd hate to have to deny it."

"Does this mean I can finally kiss you at the ceremony?"

"Let's not get ahead of ourselves." But she's still smiling as she walks away.

Will claps my shoulder. "You know the board's going to have opinions about this."

"Let them." I watch her go, the swing of her platinum hair, the confidence in her stride. "Some things are worth the hassle."

"Yeah?" He grins. "Like what?"

"Like finally getting to write happy love songs."

His laugh follows me out of the room. For the first time in twenty years, I'm leaving a press conference steady on my feet, clear in my head, and absolutely certain about where I'm going.

Right where I've always been heading.

Right to her.

Later, when it's just us in her office, I show her how worn the engraving has become on the stainless steel guitar pick from ten years of worrying it between my fingers.

"You kept it." Her voice is soft with wonder. "Through everything?"

"My good luck charm. My reminder. My..." I laugh softly. "My sobriety chip before I earned the real ones."

"Chase..." She traces the worn edges. "All those years, even when..."

"Even when I was at my worst. Even in rehab. Even when I thought I'd lost you forever." I fold her fingers around it. "Some things you just know you have to hold onto."

Her laugh is everything I've ever tried to capture in melody.

Some songs don't need to be written. They just need to be lived.

Don't Stop the Devil

ELIZA

"YOUR PHONE IS BLOWING UP," Chase observes from my office couch, where he's sprawled with an amused smile. "Mine too."

"Mute it," I mutter, staring at my laptop screen. Every industry blog is running with the story. Photos from the shoot splashed across headlines, intercut with footage from the press conference. That clip from the Grammys is trending again – Chase kissing me on his way to accept Album of the Year, leaving me stunned in my seat as he took the stage.

Michelle bursts in without knocking. "Okay, so TMZ is running with 'Rock's Greatest Love Story Finally Confirmed.' *Billboard's* going with something more tasteful about your professional history. *Rolling Stone* wants an exclusive interview—"

"No," Chase and I say in unison.

She grins. "God, you two are cute. Oh, and Justin's on line one."

I grab the phone before she's finished speaking. Chase sits up, watching me with soft eyes.

"Mom?" Justin sounds like he's trying not to laugh. "So that was quite a press conference."

"Shouldn't you be at rehearsal?"

"Are you kidding? The whole band's watching. You're all over social media. Also, that Grammy kiss is everywhere again." He pauses. "You know, when you told me Chase was finally clean, I had a feeling everything was about to change. Didn't expect him to announce it to the whole industry though."

I glance at Chase, who has the grace to look sheepish. "Yes, well..."

"I'm happy for you," Justin says softly. "Both of you. It's about damn time."

"Thank you, baby. How's the new song coming?"

"Better than my love life, apparently. Although watching you two might give me some good material."

"Goodbye, Justin."

His laugh follows me as I hang up. Chase raises an eyebrow. "Everything okay?"

"Apparently my son's going to write songs about us."

He throws his head back laughing just as Michelle returns, tablet in hand.

"The board wants an emergency meeting," she announces.

"No current contract with the band," I remind her. "No conflict of interest."

"Oh, I know. I already sent them a very detailed email about that. Also reminded them that you two, ahem… maintained perfect professional boundaries for fifteen years while he actually was signed to the label." She smirks. "Even included a spreadsheet of the band's profit margins under your management."

"I love you," I tell her seriously.

"I know. Also, Will's on his way up. Something about Chase owing him money?"

Chase groans. "I may have bet him I'd never have the guts to go public."

"When did you make this bet?"

"2006?"

I shake my head, but can't help smiling. My phone buzzes again – more board members, industry contacts, probably some press. I ignore it in favor of watching Chase read something on his own phone, his smile growing.

"What?"

Chase holds up his screen. It's an old article about the Grammy incident, with a new comment from Mark: *About time these two stopped pretending. Though after that Grammy kiss, who were they really fooling? #IndustrysBestKeptSecret #NotSoSecret*

"I still can't believe you did that," I say, remembering the shock of his lips on mine, the roar of the crowd. "No warning, no hint..."

"You're lucky that's all I did. I had this whole speech planned about how *Off the Record* was really about—"

"Don't you dare finish that sentence."

"What? Everyone knows that one's about you. The studio at 3 AM? The black dress with the broken zipper?"

Michelle clears her throat. We both start – I'd forgotten she was still there.

"As adorable as this is," she says, "we should probably draft a proper statement. Something professional about—"

My office door bursts open again. Will strides in, hand already out. "Pay up, Avery. Eighteen years of interest on that bet."

Chase pulls out his wallet, grumbling. "You know, technically the bet was that I'd never tell her how I felt in public. The Grammy kiss should have counted."

"The Grammy kiss was a drunken impulse that you both played off as theatrical," Will counters. "This was a sober confession of twenty years of love. Very different thing."

"He's got you there," I agree.

Chase hands over what looks like several hundred dollars, then points at Will. "You knew. When I made that bet, you knew this would happen eventually."

"Course I did." Will pockets the money with a grin. "Who do you think's been listening to both of you pine for each other for two decades?"

My phone rings again. The board chairman's number.

"Want me to answer it?" Michelle offers.

I look at Chase, still arguing with Will about the terms of their ancient bet. At Michelle, fiercely protective and obviously delighted. At my screen filling with messages of support from industry friends who've watched our saga play out for years.

"No," I decide. "Let it go to voicemail. I'm busy having a personal life."

Chase's head whips around, his smile brilliant. "Yeah?"

"Yeah." I stand, gathering my things. "In fact, I think I'm done for the day. The industry can wait until tomorrow to hear how we're going to 'handle' this."

"Ms. Kerr," he says, all fake scandal. "Are you playing hooky?"

"Mr. Avery," I match his tone, "I believe I am. Any objections?"

He's already reaching for his jacket. Will and Michelle exchange knowing looks.

"I'll handle the board," Michelle says. "You two... handle whatever this is."

"Twenty years of foreplay?" Will suggests.

"Out," I point at the door. "Both of you."

Their laughter follows us down the hall. Chase's hand finds mine as we wait for the elevator.

"You sure about this?" he asks softly. "Leaving the chaos for them to handle?"

I watch our joined reflection in the elevator doors like I always have, but now it's different. It's out in the open. "The chaos will still be there tomorrow. Right now..." I squeeze his hand. "Right now I just want to be us."

His smile is better than any headline.

"Us," he repeats. "I like the sound of that."

The elevator arrives with a soft ding. We step in together, leaving the industry explosion behind us.

Sacred Place

~

CHASE

ROCKET MORTGAGE FIELDHOUSE in Cleveland smells like new paint and old dreams. The massive space echoes with sound check chatter, guitar tuning, drum tests. Familiar voices in an unfamiliar setting.

"This transition's still rough," Jake Townsend says, running a hand over his tied-back blonde hair. His eyes dart between his notes and the exits – classic Jake, always mapping escape routes.

"We'll get it," Ryan Crawford answers with that easy smile that's made him Indigo King's famous frontman. "The key change from *Off the Record* into *Burning Bridges* is tricky, but—"

"But worth it," Will cuts in. "You should have heard Chase try to sing it the first time around. At least you guys are sober for the attempt."

Jude Lockwood, Indigo King's bassist, laughs

from where he's slouched against his amp. "That's setting the bar pretty low, man."

It's all surreal – watching other singers take on my songs, while actual rock legends mill around the arena. I just passed Robert Plant in the hallway. Jimmy Page is supposedly around here somewhere. And tomorrow night, we join their ranks.

"Alright," Ryan says, adjusting his mic. "From the top?"

The opening notes of *Off the Record* fill the space. Ryan's voice brings something new to the lyrics – a softness I never managed when I was writing about that night in the studio, about a black dress with a broken zipper and possibilities I was too scared to grab.

The transition hits and Jake takes over, his rougher edge perfect for *Burning Bridges*. The song I wrote when I thought I'd lost her for good. When I was too drunk and stupid to see what I was throwing away.

Then it's my turn.

Caught between silence and screaming...

Whispered Truths feels different now. No more hiding its meaning. No more pretending it isn't about steel grey eyes and purple-tipped hair and twenty years of almost.

I spot Eliza in the wings, watching. No need to

hide her presence anymore. No need to pretend these aren't all her songs. Every word, every note, every memory laid bare for everyone to hear.

When we finish, there's a moment of pure silence before the scattered crew burst into applause.

"Damn," Jake says softly. "That's gonna kill tomorrow night."

Will catches my eye across the stage. *You good?* his look asks. I nod. Better than good.

"That's a wrap for now," our stage manager calls out. "Final rehearsal's at seven. Get some rest, get some food, be ready to run the whole show tonight."

Eliza materializes beside me as I'm setting down my bass. "That sounded incredible."

"Yeah?" I can't help grinning. "Not too weird hearing other people sing our stuff?"

"Perfect choices, actually." She glances at her watch. "We've got several hours until final rehearsal. Want to get out of here for a bit?"

Ten minutes later, we're driving through Rocky River Reservation, autumn colors blazing against a perfect blue sky. Eliza's at the wheel – some habits die hard – while I watch gold and crimson leaves dance in our wake. The valley spreads out below us, the river catching late afternoon sun.

"You know what's crazy?" I say, rolling down the window to breathe in October air. "Tomorrow night, we're being inducted into the actual Hall of Fame. Us. That same band you found at the Viper Room."

"The same band that sold out stadiums," she reminds me. "The same band that changed rock music for a decade."

"Still." I shake my head. "Robert Plant is going to be there. *Robert fucking Plant.* And we're one of the youngest bands ever inducted. With all original members."

She laughs. "I saw you nearly walk into a wall when you passed him earlier."

"I maintained my dignity."

"You absolutely did not."

We pull over at Huntington Reservation, Cleveland spread out below us, Lake Erie stretching endless and blue beyond. Urban architecture meets autumn trees meets infinite horizon. Eliza kills the engine but makes no move to get out.

"What are you thinking?" I ask softly.

"I'm thinking about hearing those songs in order like that. Our whole story laid out in three acts." She turns to face me. "The beginning, the middle, and now... now we finally get the ending right."

"Not an ending," I say, taking her hand. "Just a better beginning."

Her fingers lace with mine. "I like the sound of that."

The sun starts to set, painting everything in shades of gold and crimson. Tomorrow, we'll join rock's immortals. Tomorrow, I'll hear other voices tell parts of our story before I finally tell the end myself. Tomorrow, everything changes.

But right now, watching autumn leaves dance past our windshield, holding the hand of the woman who believed in me before I believed in myself, I realize something:

Everything that matters already has.

"We should head back soon," Eliza says eventually. "Get some dinner before final rehearsal."

"Five more minutes?" I'm not ready to share her yet. Not ready to be Chase Avery, Hall of Fame inductee. I just want to be Chase, watching leaves fall with Eliza.

Her smile is soft. "Five more minutes."

Somewhere in the distance, church bells chime. A perfect October evening spreads out before us. Tonight we'll run the whole show, tomorrow brings all its ceremony and grandeur, but this moment...

This is the one I want to remember.

Can't Quench the Fire

ELIZA

THE PRIVATE DINING room at Giovanni's overlooks downtown Cleveland, city lights twinkling like earthbound stars. Chase fidgets with his water glass, that tell I've known for twenty years. He wants to say something but isn't sure how.

"Out with it," I say, smiling. "You've been sitting on something all day."

He laughs softly. "That obvious?"

"Only to me."

He reaches for his jacket, pulls out a small notebook – the kind he always used for lyrics. My heart skips.

"I've been writing again," he says quietly. "Real writing, not just... not like before. Different stuff. Clearer." He pauses. "Better."

"Yeah?"

"Yeah." His fingers trace the notebook's edges.

"Will and Mark have been coming by the house. Playing around with some arrangements. It feels... it feels right. For the first time in years."

The implications hover between us like smoke. I take a sip of water, choosing my words carefully.

"Have you talked to them? About making it official?"

"Not yet. Wanted to talk to you first." His green eyes meet mine. "For obvious reasons."

A waiter appears with our appetizers. We wait until he's gone before continuing.

"The industry's changed," I say. "Streaming, social media, virtual concerts. It's not the same land- scape you left."

"Good thing I know the President of a major label." His smile is tentative. "One who's pretty good at navigating changing landscapes."

And there it is.

"Chase..."

"I know." He reaches for my hand. "I know it's complicated. But hear me out? Please?"

I nod.

"What if... what if we did it differently this time? Same label, different management team. Michelle's been grooming that new guy – James? He's got a good track record. And you've got other artists to focus on. Bigger picture stuff."

"You've thought about this."

"Haven't stopped thinking about it." He squeezes

my fingers. "The music's different now. I'm different. No more addiction metaphors or pain songs or... or loving you from a distance. This is..." He smiles. "This is what happy sounds like."

"And Will and Mark? They're ready for this?"

"They've been ready. Just waiting for me to get my shit together." He pulls his hand back, runs it through his hair. "Look, I know it's asking a lot. The band signing with Blackmore again while we're together. But maybe that's exactly why it could work. No more pretending. No more blurred lines. Everything professional stays professional. Everything personal stays personal."

"Like we did such a good job of that before," I can't help teasing.

"But that's just it – we did. For fifteen years, through all our... our mess, the band never suffered from it. The label never suffered. If anything, any suffering was caused by *me*. We kept those lines clear even when everything else was chaos." He leans forward. "We're better at this now. Smarter. More mature."

"Says the man who just announced our relationship to the entire industry without warning."

His laugh is warm. "Okay, slightly more mature."

I study him in the candlelight. The clarity in his eyes. The steady hands. The man I always knew he could be.

"James is good," I say slowly. "One of our best

up-and-coming managers. But he's never handled a band of your caliber."

"Perfect time to learn, then." His smile widens. "While we're learning too. How to do this right. All of it."

"The board will have opinions."

"The board always has opinions. But they also like profits. And an Incendiary Ink comeback? Sober, stable, with fresh material?" He raises an eyebrow. "That's profit waiting to happen."

He's right. Of course, he's right.

"You're really ready for this?" I ask softly. "All of it? The pressure, the publicity, the scrutiny? Especially now that we're public?"

"I'm ready for anything." His hand finds mine again. "As long as I get to come home to you at the end of it."

The city lights shimmer beyond the window. Twenty years of history pulse between us. But for the first time, the future feels brighter than the past.

"Play me something?" I ask. "Just a taste?"

He pulls out his phone, hands me an earbud. "Rough demo. Will recorded it last week."

The opening notes fill my ear – something new, something bright. Something that sounds like hope and healing and love finally getting it right.

"It's beautiful," I whisper.

"It's yours." He smiles. "They all are. They always were."

Tomorrow brings the ceremony, the induction, the weight of history. But right now, sharing earbuds in a candlelit room while new music plays between us, we're just Chase and Eliza.

Finally figuring out how to be both.

'Cause I Know You're the One

CHASE

"IF YOU ADJUST those rings one more time," Will says from the hotel suite's couch, his leather jacket creaking as he leans back, "I'm going to throw them out the window."

"They need to be in the right order."

"They're fine," Mark calls from the bathroom, where he's trying to get his shirt cuffs to show off his sleeves just right. "Unlike my hair, which is refusing to cooperate."

"Your hair hasn't cooperated since 1998," Will shoots back, spinning a drumstick between his fingers.

The suite buzzes with pre-ceremony energy. Mark's array of hair products covering every flat surface. My black Alexander McQueen suit with its subtle silver threading laid out like armor. Will's custom leather pieces and Mark's strategically ripped designer wear waiting their turn.

My phone buzzes. A text from Justin.

> JUSTIN: Mom looks incredible. You're gonna lose your mind.

Another buzz. Michelle this time.

> MICHELLE: Ready to make Rolling Stone's best dressed list, rockstar?

"Cars are here," Mark announces, finally emerging. "How's the—"

"If you ask about your hair, I'm disowning you," Will cuts in, silver chains clinking as he stands.

The elevator ride down is a blur of anticipation. Tonight we join the immortals. Tonight we play our biggest songs with Ryan, Jude, and Jake. Tonight...

The elevator doors open, and I forget how to breathe.

Eliza stands in the hotel lobby in a black Versace that somehow manages to be both elegant and dangerous – strategic cutouts and leather panels that make her look like the rock queen she is. The purple in her hair seems almost electric against the black. She turns, and that smile – the one I've seen across recording studios and board rooms and venue halls for twenty years – hits me full force.

"Damn," Will whispers appreciatively.

I cross to her, not caring who sees. Not having to care anymore.

"You look..." Words fail me.

"Back at you." Her fingers trace the metallic threads in my jacket. "Very rock 'n' roll royalty."

"Does that make you my queen?"

"That makes me the woman who's about to steal your thunder at your own Hall of Fame induction."

She's right. She's absolutely right.

"I can live with that."

The red carpet stretches before us like a crimson river. Cameras flash. The real music press is out in force – *Rolling Stone, Spin, Billboard*. But for once, I'm not focused on any of it.

"Ready?" she asks softly.

I take her hand. "Born ready."

The moment we step onto the carpet, it's chaos. Beautiful chaos. The band forms up around us – Will and Mark, our guard of honor. The photographers go wild for our collective look – leather and metal and attitude with just enough polish to show why we're here.

"Chase! Eliza! How about one for Rolling Stone?"

"Rock's power couple!"

"Band shot!"

"Just the two of you!"

She fits perfectly against my side, like she was always meant to be there. Every pose feels natural. Every smile real.

"Incendiary Ink!" Jan from *Spin* calls out. "How's it feel joining the ranks of rock gods?"

"Like we've still got more noise to make," Will answers with a wicked grin.

"Any truth to the comeback rumors?" Spinner from *Billboard* this time.

"We'll see." I look at Eliza, see my own joy reflected in steel grey eyes. "Some things are worth waiting for."

The cameras love that. Love us. Love the way she laughs when I whisper lyrics just for her. The way the band clusters protectively around us, years of friendship on display.

"Looking good!" Someone shouts. I turn to find Jake in his signature leather pants, Ryan and Jude beside him in their own takes on rock formal. More photos. More poses. The next generation of Blackmore talent celebrating with us.

"Save some chemistry for the after-party," Michelle teases as she passes in her own edgy designer wear.

But I can't help it. Can't stop looking at Eliza. Can't believe I get to do this – really do this – hold her hand in public, kiss her cheek for the cameras, show the world what I've known for twenty years:

She's the best thing that ever happened to me. To any of us.

"Speech ready?" she asks as we near the end of the carpet.

"Better be. I've only had twenty years to write it."

Her laugh is everything. The cameras catch it, that perfect moment of joy. Of us. Of *finally*.

"Let's go make history," Will says, chains jingling as he claps my shoulder.

Eliza squeezes my hand. The band surrounds us. The doors to rock immortality wait ahead.

Time to show the world what we're made of.

All of us.

Together.

Heaven's Got a Back Door

ELIZA

THE PODIUM FEELS electric under my fingers. Two thousand people in the audience, but I only see three. Will, steady as his own drumbeat. Mark, fingers probably itching for his guitar. And Chase.

"Twenty years ago," I begin, my voice steady despite my racing heart, "I walked into the Viper Room on a Tuesday night. Rock music was at a crossroads. Grunge had faded, leaving a vacuum no one knew how to fill. The industry was drowning in manufactured pop, boy bands were ruling the charts, and everyone was searching for the next big sound, the next movement, the next revolution. I wasn't supposed to be there that night – had an early meeting the next day. But something made me stay. Something in the air. Something in the sound."

The room is silent, waiting.

"What I heard that night wasn't just music. It

wasn't grunge, wasn't pop-punk, wasn't emo, wasn't anything that had come before. It was revolution. It was evolution. It was three guys from nowhere who were about to change everything."

I find Will's eyes. "A drummer who could make your heart beat in time with his." Mark's turn. "A guitarist who painted colors with sound." Finally, Chase. "And a frontman who wrote poetry like punch lines and played bass like warfare."

Scattered applause, quickly hushed.

"Incendiary Ink didn't just make music. They made magic. They made history. When everyone else was trying to replicate what had come before, they created something entirely new. Nine platinum albums. Sixteen sold-out world tours. Over fifty million records sold. But numbers don't tell the real story."

I gesture to where Murderous Crows and Indigo King sit. "The real story is in every band they inspired. Every artist who heard them and thought 'I want to do that.' Every kid who picked up a guitar because of Mark's solos. Every drummer who tried to match Will's rhythms. Every songwriter who studied Chase's lyrics like scripture."

Movement catches my eye – Chase shifting in his seat, and my heart stutters momentarily.

"The real story is in their survival. Three original members, twenty years, one vision. Through every up and down. Every triumph and tragedy. Every almost and finally."

The industry crowd stirs at that last word. They know what it means now.

"I've watched this band grow from dive bar darlings to stadium gods. I've seen them fight and fall and rise and soar. I've seen them break records and break hearts. I've seen them define an entire era of rock music, creating a sound that became the blueprint for a generation of bands that followed."

My voice softens. "And through it all, they've remained exactly who they are: three guys from nowhere who changed everything."

Chase's eyes lock with mine. Twenty years of history passes between us in a heartbeat.

"Tonight, Incendiary Ink joins the immortals. Their names will be written in rock history forever. But for those of us who were there... for those of us who heard that first chord in that dim club on a Tuesday night, when rock music was searching for its future... they've been immortal all along."

I grip the podium tighter and smile directly at Chase as the lights dim for a video showing the band's history on the big screen behind me. I turn to watch the package the label put together, letting myself get caught up in the past for a moment before I have to continue my speech. Once the video ends, I have to wipe at my eyes as the nostalgia of it all gets to me. I clear my throat, and the crowd chuckles softly with me as I gather myself enough to go on.

"They say every great band has a secret weapon. Something that sets them apart. Incendiary Ink's wasn't their sound, though that was revolutionary. Wasn't their style, though that was iconic. It wasn't even their talent, though that was undeniable."

Will grins, knowing where this is going.

"Their secret weapon was truth. Raw, honest, uncompromising truth. In every lyric. Every note. Every performance. When the industry was churning out manufactured hits, they gave us authentic emotion. When music was losing its edge, they gave us something sharp enough to cut. They never pretended to be anything but exactly who they were. And who they were... who they *are*... is quite simply one of the greatest rock bands of all time."

The audience erupts. I wait for it to quiet.

"So, it is my profound honor, both as President of Blackmore Records and as someone who has loved this band in every way possible, to officially welcome Incendiary Ink into the Rock and Roll Hall of Fame."

The standing ovation is immediate. Through the thunder of applause, I see Chase mouth three words that make my heart stop.

Will and Mark embrace him, their own eyes suspiciously bright. The industry photographers go wild. Somewhere in the crowd, I hear Michelle whoop.

But all I see is Chase, looking at me like I've just given him every dream he's ever had.

Maybe I have.

The band makes their way to the stage. There will be other speeches – their acceptance, their performance still to come. But this moment...

This perfect moment of pride and joy and love finally spoken aloud...

This is ours.

Forever.

Heart Beat Here

THE OPENING RIFF of *Burning Bridges* fills the arena as we make our way to the stage. Will's already grinning – this was his favorite to play live, the one that first got crowds really moving with us.

He takes the podium first, spinning a drumstick casually.

"So, funny story. Twenty years ago, we're playing the Viper Room on a Tuesday night, probably breaking at least three fire codes with our equipment setup, when this woman in killer heels walks up to us after a show and hands us a business card. Takes one look at us and says 'You're either going to be the biggest band in the world or the biggest disaster I've ever seen.' Turns out, we were both."

Perfect timing, perfect delivery. The crowd loves it. I spot Ryan and Jake in the audience, nodding – they've heard this story, lived their own version of it.

"Six months later we're opening at the Wiltern, blowing the power during our first song. A year after that, we're selling out Madison Square Garden, and I still can't believe they let us near the electrical system." He grins. "Twenty years, nine platinum albums, and only minimal property damage later, here we are."

The laughter is warm, appreciative. Industry veterans who remember those early shows are nodding.

"Thank you to everyone who got us here. Our families, our crew, our fans. And especially to Eliza Kerr, who saw something worth betting on in three guys who couldn't even properly run a soundcheck. Even if two-thirds of us were usually late to meetings."

Mark takes his place next, running a hand through his eternally uncooperative hair.

"Music..." he starts, then has to clear his throat. "Music saved my life. These guys saved my life. We were just kids trying to make noise that meant something. Trying to carve out our own sound when everyone said guitar music was dead. Trying to say something that mattered when everyone said rock had said it all."

He grips the podium. "That first tour, playing to half-empty clubs, we'd watch the crowd slowly get it. Watch them feel what we were trying to do. Something different. Something new. And somehow...

somehow that noise reached people. Changed people. Changed us."

I see Jake watching intently – he was one of those kids in those crowds, before Murderous Crows was even an idea.

"To every kid out there making noise in their garage – keep going. Keep playing. Keep believing. Sometimes the most beautiful sounds come from the most broken places. And to Ryan, Jake, Jude, all the bands coming up now – keep pushing it forward. Keep making it yours. Thank you."

Then it's my turn.

The walk to the podium feels like twenty years condensed into twenty steps. Everything we've been through. Everything we've become.

"What do you say," I begin as the crowd goes quiet, "when your dreams come true? When the impossible becomes reality? When three guys from nowhere end up somewhere they never dared imagine?"

The spotlight feels warm on my face. Grounding.

"You say thank you. To our families who supported us. Our crew who kept us running. Our fans who kept believing. The industry that gave us a chance. And..." I find her in the group of people standing behind us, steel grey eyes bright with tears. "And to one person in particular."

The room goes silent.

"Eliza Kerr. You didn't just discover us. You didn't

just sign us. You believed in us before we believed in ourselves. You saw what we could be before we knew how to be it. You protected us, guided us, fought for us. And personally..." My voice catches. "Personally, you saved me. More times than I can count. In more ways than I can say."

Will's hand finds my shoulder, steadying me.

"Everyone knows our story now. The ups and downs. The almosts and finallys. But what they might not know is that every song – every single one – was trying to say what I couldn't. What I can finally say now, in front of everyone: I love you. I've loved you for twenty years. And being inducted into the Hall of Fame wouldn't mean anything if you weren't here to share it."

The room erupts. I see Michelle dabbing her eyes. Justin whooping from his seat.

"To everyone else – thank you. For the support, the faith, the love. To my brothers..." I turn to Will and Mark. "We did it. We actually fucking did it. And we're not done yet."

The crowd catches that hint about the future, murmurs rising. I see Ryan and Jake exchange knowing looks – they've heard the new demos, know what's coming.

"Rock and roll isn't just about music. It's about truth. About heart. About love and loss and finding your way home. Tonight, we join the immortals. Tonight, we become part of rock history. But the best part? The best part is we get to share it with everyone who got us here. Everyone who believed. Everyone who stayed."

Michelle is full-on crying now. Justin's got that proud smile that looks just like his mother's. And Eliza...

I lock eyes with her one last time.

"Everyone who finally got their timing right."

The standing ovation drowns out everything else. Will and Mark envelope me in a group hug. Photographers go crazy. But all I see is her – the woman who first believed in our sound, who protected our vision, who saved my life, who waited twenty years for me to get it right.

Some dreams take longer to come true.

But they're worth every second of the wait.

Whispered Truths

ELIZA

RYAN TAKES *Off the Record* first, his easy charm bringing fresh life to a song I've known since its birth in that late-night studio session. Jake follows with *Burning Bridges*, his rougher edge perfect for its angry heartbreak. The crowd is loving all of it, and I can't help but feel the energy of the room lift to levels I don't think we've seen tonight.

Then the lights dim.

A single spotlight finds Chase as the opening notes of *Whispered Truths* fill the arena, and the crowd goes crazy. My heart stops as his eyes find mine. This song - this song I've heard a thousand times, that I've watched crowds sing back to him in stadiums across the world, that I never knew...

In the silence between words,
In the spaces we don't fill,

There's a truth we've never heard,
A promise we can't fulfill...

Oh god. Every board meeting. Every studio session. Every time we chose silence over truth. My hands start shaking as the next verse strips away years of carefully crafted denial.

Drowning in expectations,
Reaching out as we both fall,
Every single complication
Echoes down this empty hall.

The crowd joins in on the chorus, thousands of voices singing our pain back to us. Michelle grabs my hand as the sound washes over me - all these people, all these years, singing about us without knowing. The way he's looking at me now, no substances dulling his eyes, no pretense left between us...

Whispered truths that we can't face,
Holding on just to let go,
Trading tomorrow for some kind of grace,
Always pretending not to know.

Not to know...

Tears blur my vision. I remember when this song first hit the charts. Remember watching him perform it at the Grammys, thinking it was just another brilliant piece of songwriting. Never realizing he wrote it after a night I told him we needed clearer boundaries. After I chose the label's interests over him. After I...

The arena is deafening now, every voice lifted in a chorus I finally understand. Through the wall of sound, through the tears, through years of mystery finally solved, Chase's eyes hold mine. Singing our story to the world. Singing it to me.

Finally.

The Night Cries Out
(For You)

CHASE

BLACKMORE KNOWS how to throw a party. The top floor of Cleveland's tallest hotel has been transformed into rock 'n' roll heaven - open bar, classic vinyl spinning between live sets, and enough industry elite to fill a Hall of Fame ceremony all over again.

"You two," Michelle says, appearing with champagne for Eliza, "are trending worldwide. Apparently, that performance broke the internet."

Eliza laughs against my shoulder. She hasn't left my side all night, and I'm not complaining. "Please tell me you have PR handling it."

"Honey, I have PR handling the PR who's handling it." Michelle grins. "Now come on, people are waiting to congratulate the happy couple. Both on the induction and the obviously-not-news news."

We make our rounds. Robert Plant himself tells us

it was "about bloody time on both counts." Jake and Ryan hold court by the bar, already planning future collaborations. Will and Mark are surrounded by admirers, telling increasingly exaggerated stories about our early days.

"Remember when you used to have to stand on opposite sides of the room at these things?" Justin appears, looking every inch the rock star himself. "The whole 'professional distance' act?"

"Your mother was better at it than I was," I admit.

"Please." Eliza squeezes my hand. "You're the one who kept finding reasons to cross the room."

"Speaking of crossing rooms..." Michelle's voice carries that dangerous edge of plotting. "They're about to play *Whispered Truths*. You two should definitely dance to that."

Before we can protest, the opening notes fill the space. Eliza's eyes meet mine, and suddenly we're back in that studio years ago, when I first played her the rough cut at 3 AM.

"May I?" I ask formally, making her laugh.

"Always."

The dance floor clears for us. No more pretending this isn't our song. No more maintaining professional distance. Just us, swaying to the music that started it all.

"Been waiting twenty years to dance with you properly," I murmur in her ear.

"Pretty sure you danced with me at that industry party in '08."

"Pretty sure I was trying to make you jealous by dancing with someone else."

"Pretty sure it worked."

The song shifts to *Burning Bridges*. Ryan grabs Jake, dramatically recreating our earlier performance. The dance floor fills with industry elite letting loose. Through the chaos, I spot Will giving us a thumbs up while Mark pretends to wipe away tears.

"Come here," I say, pulling Eliza toward a quieter corner. The city spreads out below us, lights twinkling like earthbound stars.

"Quite a night," she says softly.

"Quite a twenty years."

She turns in my arms, facing me. "Was it worth the wait?"

"Every second." I brush back a strand of purple-tipped platinum. "Though I wouldn't mind not waiting anymore."

"No?"

"No." I kiss her temple. "I've got some new songs to record. Need a label President's opinion on them."

Her laugh vibrates against my chest. "I might know someone. Though I hear she's dating a rockstar now."

"Lucky guy."

"Lucky girl."

The party swirls around us - Michelle directing photographers to "capture the moment," Justin showing Will something on his phone, Mark deep in conversation with Robert Plant of all people. But here in our corner, it's just us.

"Eliza?"

"Hmm?"

"I love you. In case that wasn't clear from the very public declarations and worldwide trending topics."

She kisses me, right there in front of everyone. No hiding. No pretending. No professional distance.

"I love you too. In case that wasn't clear from the last twenty years."

"Crystal clear." I pull her closer as *Off the Record* starts playing. "Want to dance to yet another one of our songs? Now that everyone knows they're our songs?"

Her smile is everything I've ever tried to capture in melody.

"Lead the way, rockstar."

The night spins on, a blur of celebration and congratulations and joy. But all I feel is her hand in mine, all I see is steel grey eyes and purple-tipped platinum, all I hear is the music that brought us together and the truth we're finally free to speak.

Everything about today I once thought was impossible. The band. The induction. Eliza. Never in my wildest dreams did I ever think things could be this good. I used to buckle under pressure that wasn't even there. I created all of my own demons. But I've also fought them.

Today, it feels like I won.

Never Tear Us Apart

ELIZA

THE FIRST THING I register is sunlight warming my face. The second is Chase's gaze.

"How long have you been watching me sleep?" I murmur, not opening my eyes.

"Long enough to memorize every beautiful detail." His fingers trace my cheekbone, trail down my neck. "Though I've been doing that for twenty years."

I blink awake to find him propped on one elbow beside me, hair adorably mussed, eyes dark with want.

"Last night was real?" I ask, though the delicious ache in my feet from dancing until dawn answers that question.

"All of it." He brushes back my hair, then follows the path with his lips. "The induction, the performance, the party..." His smile turns wicked. "The way you kissed me in front of the entire industry."

"Seemed appropriate after your speech."

"Seemed perfect." His mouth finds that spot below my ear that makes me gasp. "You're perfect."

Heat pools low in my belly as his hands map familiar territory. "Chase..."

"Do you know," he murmurs against my throat, "how many times I've dreamed of this? Just us. No rush." His teeth graze my pulse point. "No bound-aries." His hand slides lower. "No holding back."

I arch into his touch, my body remembering every secret he's learned over twenty years. "Show me."

He takes his time, using everything he knows about my body to drive me wild. The spot on my hip that makes me shiver. The way I arch when he kisses that sensitive place on my inner thigh.

"Please," I breathe, pulling him up to me.

"Twenty years," he says against my lips. "Twenty years of wanting you like this."

When he finally moves inside me, it's with the perfect rhythm he's always had. *Bass player's timing*, I used to tease. Now his tempo builds steadily, delib-erately, until I'm gasping his name.

"Look at me," he commands softly. "Let me see you."

Steel grey meets green as everything shatters. He follows right after, my name a low groan in his throat.

After, he gathers me close, both of us catching our breath.

"I could get used to this," I murmur, tracing patterns on his chest.

"Planning to." He catches my hand, kisses each finger. "Think the industry would notice if we just stayed in bed forever?"

"Probably." I smile against his skin. "But they've had twenty years of professional us. They can wait a little longer."

His answering laugh vibrates through me. Perfect rhythm, perfect timing.

Finally.

What Are You Waiting For

CHASE

THE HEADLINES START ROLLING in over room service coffee: *"Rock's Greatest Love Story Finally Confirmed!" "Hall of Fame Inductees Incendiary Ink Steal Their Own Show" "Twenty Years in the Making: Inside Music's Most Secret Romance."*

"Your phone's about to explode," Eliza observes from the suite's plush couch, still in my t-shirt from last night. Cleveland radio plays *Burning Bridges* in the background - for the umpteenth time this morning. "Will says Twitter or whatever it's called now is losing its mind over the performance."

"Let it." I hand her fresh coffee, peek at her laptop screen. *Rolling Stone*'s review of the ceremony is overwhelmingly positive. Our award from last night sits on the coffee table, catching morning light filtered through Cleveland's autumn clouds. "Oh look, we're 'rock's most compelling comeback story.'"

"Speaking of comeback..." She gives me that look I've known for twenty years. "Three messages from Atlantic. Two from Sony. Even Universal's sniffing around. All since the ceremony ended."

"Hoping to steal us from Blackmore?"

"Can't steal what isn't signed." But her smile is soft. "Though a certain label President might have an inside track."

My phone buzzes again. A text from Mark this time.

> MARK: Dude. Ryan and Jake want to collaborate on the new stuff. Also your love life is trending higher than our actual induction. Congrats? Also what time's your flight? Will's trying to change his to match.

"The vultures are circling," I muse, settling beside her. Lake Erie stretches grey and endless beyond our window. "Though I'm more interested in a certain label's opinion of our demos."

"Mixing business with pleasure already?"

"Always have." I kiss her temple. "We're just honest about it now."

She closes her laptop, turns to face me fully. "Chase... are you sure? About Blackmore? We could keep business and personal separate this time. No one would blame you for signing elsewhere."

"Hey." I take her hands. "Twenty years we've

proven we can handle both. The only difference now is we don't have to pretend we're not in love while doing it."

Her phone chimes. She glances at it and laughs. "Michelle says the board is having an emergency meeting about 'recent developments' as soon as we land in LA tomorrow."

"Bet they love that their President is trending worldwide."

"Bet they love that their potential new signing is the reason why."

I pull her closer, breathing in her familiar scent mixed with lingering traces of last night's celebration. "Any regrets? About going public?"

"Only that we waited so long." She traces my jaw. "Though maybe we needed the time. To get here. To get it right."

Another buzz. Justin this time.

> JUSTIN: You two seen the memes yet? Also, TMZ has photos of you leaving the party together. Mom, your hair looks amazing even at 4am. Unfair.

"We're going to have to release a statement eventually," she sighs. "Something official."

"How about 'Mind your own fucking business, we're busy being happy'?"

Her laugh echoes through the suite. "Very Presidential."

"Very honest."

More notifications flood in. Will sending screenshots of fan reactions. Michelle with PR strategies. Mark with potential studio dates for when we're back in LA. The future rushing at us like a freight train.

But for now...

For now we're just us. Finally us. Room service coffee and headlines and twenty years of almosts turned into definitely.

"Move in with me," I say suddenly.

She pulls back, eyes wide. "What?"

"When we get home. Move in with me. Or I'll move in with you. Or we'll buy a new place together. I don't care. I just... I'm done with separate spaces. Separate lives. I want to wake up with you every morning. Want to read ridiculous headlines over coffee. Want..." I cup her face. "I want everything. With you. Finally."

Her smile is brighter than any spotlight I've ever stood in.

"Yes."

"Yeah?"

"Yeah." She kisses me softly. "Though we might want to wait until after the press dies down to go house hunting."

"Probably smart." I pull her back against me,

watching clouds drift over Lake Erie. "Good thing I know this incredibly smart label President. She always knows the right timing."

Her laugh is better than any song I've ever written.

Some headlines write themselves.

Some truths don't need to be whispered anymore.

Look At Me Now

ELIZA

WALKING into Blackmore Records holding Chase's hand feels surreal. Like crossing a line I've policed for twenty years. The security guard, Manny, who's watched us maintain "professional distance" since the Clinton administration, can't hide his grin. The receptionist's eyes go wide as she fumbles her "Welcome back, Ms. Kerr, Mr. Avery." By the time we reach the elevator, the entire lobby's buzzing.

"Having fun?" Chase murmurs, clearly enjoying the reactions. His thumb draws lazy circles on my palm – a gesture he used to restrict to private moments.

"Shouldn't you be meeting James right now instead of escorting me to my office?"

"Can't I do both?" He grins. "Besides, I like being able to walk you to work without having to pretend I'm here to discuss 'marketing strategies.'"

The elevator opens and Michelle's waiting, practically vibrating with glee. "Well, well, well. Look who finally learned to use the front door instead of sneaking through the garage."

"That was one time," Chase protests.

"That was at least twelve times. Karen in security kept a log." She falls into step beside us. "Board's ready when you are, boss. And James is in the small conference room preparing for his meeting about digital streaming rights, touring schedules, and how to market the comeback of the year." She winks at Chase. "Also, apparently Accounting started a betting pool years ago on when you two would finally get together. Pretty sure Janet just won enough to retire."

"Subtle," I mutter.

Every employee we pass has a different reaction. Tina from Legal gives us a knowing smirk – she had to review all those carefully worded contracts keeping business and pleasure separate. The marketing team practically squeals – they've been sitting on a "love story twenty years in the making" campaign for a decade, according to Michelle.

"Ms. Kerr," my assistant Jenna stands, professional as ever despite her barely concealed smile. "The board is gathering in ten minutes. And Mr. Avery, James asked me to remind you about your eleven o'clock discussion of publishing rights and tour logistics."

"Thank you, Jenna." I turn to Chase. "That's your

cue to go talk business with someone who isn't sleeping with you."

"Yes, ma'am." Then, because he's Chase, he kisses me right there in front of my entire department. "Dinner later? That new place on Sunset you've been wanting to try?"

"Assuming the board doesn't fire me."

"Then they'd have to sign us to a different label. Though I hear Universal's very interested in our 'evolved sound and established fanbase.'"

"Go. Talk to James."

His laugh follows him down the hall. Michelle appears at my elbow with coffee and that smirk she's perfected over two decades of watching us pine.

"The marketing team is already planning how to spin the comeback announcement," she says as we head toward the board room. "'Rock's greatest love story returns to the studio' is currently winning. Though your love life is generating more buzz than the actual music. Justin's already texted me four different memes about you two."

"Wonderful."

"Oh please, you're loving this. Oh look, a new text, Janet in Accounting says thank you. Her retirement party's next week."

"You're fucking hilarious, as always," I say, turning into my office and giving her a wicked grin as I close the door slowly between us.

The board meeting goes exactly as expected.

Concerns about conflict of interest. Questions about professional boundaries. Until finally:

"And you're certain you can maintain objectivity?" Harrison peers at me over his glasses. "The streaming rights alone for their back catalog—"

"I maintained it for fifteen years while they were actually signed to us," I remind him. "Through nine platinum albums and a very public Grammy kiss. The only difference now is I don't have to pretend not to care about their frontman."

"And the potential signing? The 360 deal terms?"

"James will handle everything. I've already recused myself from negotiations. Though I hear their new sound is," I can't help smiling, "evolved."

"Speaking of James..." Michelle pokes her head in. "Sorry to interrupt, but he'd like you to stop by their meeting. Strictly as label President, of course. Nothing to do with the fact that your boyfriend just approved the tour schedule you secretly helped design."

The small conference room buzzes with energy. Chase, Will, and Mark sprawl in chairs while James gestures enthusiastically at a whiteboard covered in plans for digital marketing, streaming platforms, and tour dates.

"Ms. Kerr," James straightens. "Perfect timing. We were just discussing promotional strategy for the comeback album. Initial market research suggests an enormous appetite for both the new sound and the... personal narrative."

"Don't let me interrupt." I lean against the doorframe, catching Chase's eye. The way he still looks at me after twenty years makes my heart skip. "Though I have to ask - will there be any songs about secret office romances on the new album?"

"Nah," Chase grins. "Thinking of writing about being disgustingly happy instead. Will's already threatened to quit if I get too sappy."

"You're twenty years too late," Will groans. "We've been playing your love songs this whole time."

"Every. Single. Album." Mark agrees. "Though the new stuff is actually good. Less angst, more actual emotion."

"The streaming projections for the first single are incredibly promising," James soldiers on, professional despite his growing smile. "And the tour presale numbers—"

"What he means is," Will translates, "people really want to see these two make heart eyes at each other on stage now that they're allowed."

"Some of us still pine," Mark protests. "Keep the brand consistent. Though maybe fewer songs about grey eyes in this album?"

"Meeting," James reminds them. "We're having a meeting. About actual business. Publishing rights? International distribution? Anyone?"

I leave them to it, heart full. Twenty years of separating personal and professional, and now...

"They're going to be incredible," Michelle says, falling into step beside me yet again.

"Are you stalking me or something?" I glare at her sideways.

She ignores me. "The comeback album of the decade. Also, Justin says he's writing a song called *My Mom's Dating a RockStar*. Says he'll premiere it at Janet's retirement party."

"He wouldn't dare. That's a joke, right?"

"He absolutely would... but unfortunately, yeah, I think it's a joke. Oh, and TMZ wants to know if you're wearing an engagement ring in those Cleveland photos."

"Jesus Christ," I sigh, already worn out from everything hitting me all at once. "I'm not."

"Yet," she sing-songs.

I roll my eyes at her as we reach my office just as Chase's laugh echoes down the hall. The sound fits here now. Belongs here.

Just like we finally belong to each other.

Properly. Publicly. Professionally. Personally.

In broad fucking daylight.

The Best

CHASE

"LET'S take it from the second verse," Raphael's voice comes through the intercom. "Chase, try pulling back on that bass line just a touch. Let Mark's guitar breathe there."

We're four hours into today's session, working on what might be our first single. Joe adjusts something on the board while Raphael leans forward, that intense focus I remember from our last three albums.

"Rolling," Joe announces. "Take seventeen."

The new songs feel different. Cleaner. Not just because I'm sober, but because I'm finally writing from a place of peace instead of pain. No more hiding meanings in metaphors. No more disguising love songs as ballads about nameless muses.

"Cut." Raphael again. "Will, that fill in the bridge - do it again, but think about what you did in take twelve. That pocket was perfect."

"Take twelve? Really?" Will laughs, wiping his sweaty hands on a towel. "You expect me to remember that far back?"

Mark and I both turn to him in unison, smirks on our faces. "Yes. We do."

The studio door opens and Eliza appears with bags of takeout. Still in her work suit, obviously between meetings. The sight of her here, openly bringing lunch to her boyfriend's recording session, still feels like a small miracle.

"Perfect timing," Raphael says. "I need fresh ears on this bridge anyway. Thirty minutes?"

The control room fills with the rustle of takeout bags and appreciation for the break. Even James is here today, between meetings about marketing strategies and distribution deals.

"How's it going?" Eliza asks, settling beside me on the studio couch.

"Your boyfriend's being disgustingly happy in all the new songs," Will informs her, already reaching for the food. "It's terrible for our rock credibility."

"Horrible," Mark agrees around a mouthful of sandwich. "People might actually realize we're good musicians instead of just tortured artists."

"Play her the new bridge," Joe suggests from his spot by the board.

I grab my bass, start the riff we've been perfecting all morning. Eliza's eyes light up - she's always loved watching the process, even back when we had to pretend it was purely professional interest.

"That's gorgeous," she says when I finish. "The key change in the middle..."

"Told you she'd catch that," Will tells Mark. "Pay up."

"You bet on whether I'd notice the key change?"

"We bet on how fast you'd notice," Mark corrects. "Will said under ten seconds. I gave you at least thirty. Clearly underestimated your musical ear."

"Clearly underestimated how well she knows our sound," I say.

"Alright, children," Raphael cuts in, though he's smiling. "Break's over. Chase, I want to try that bass line with a different mic setup. Joe's got some ideas."

The next few hours fly by in a blur of takes and adjustments. The songs come alive under our hands - familiar enough to be Incendiary Ink, but evolved. Grown up. Like us.

"One more pass at the chorus," Raphael says around six. "Then we'll call it. Fresh ears tomorrow."

Eliza left hours ago for meetings but promised to come back. Tonight's her place. My toothbrush has a permanent spot in her bathroom, just like half her closet seems to live at my house now.

The final take flows perfectly. Everything clicking into place like it was always meant to be this way. The music, the band, the love I don't have to hide anymore.

"That's good," Raphael announces. "Really good. See you all tomorrow at ten?"

Will and Mark pack up, heading home to their own lives, their own loves. Joe starts shutting down the board while James makes one last call about distribution rights.

Eliza appears in the doorway just as I'm putting away my bass. Perfect timing, as always.

"Ready?" she asks. "I was thinking takeout and bed. I have that early board meeting, but..."

"But you sleep better when I'm there?" I finish for her.

"Exactly."

Wildfire

ELIZA

EPILOGUE

"That's the last box from my car," Chase announces, dropping it in what will become our living room. The February sun streams through floor-to-ceiling windows, painting patterns on hardwood floors we haven't filled with furniture yet. Malibu stretches out below us, ocean meeting sky in perfect blue infinity.

"My movers come tomorrow," I remind him, but I can't stop smiling. *Our house.* The moment we walked in, we both knew. The open layout perfect for entertaining Justin's band and our industry friends. The guest house Chase immediately saw as a studio. The view that made us both stop breathing.

"I still can't believe you let me put in a recording studio."

"Let you? I'm the one who suggested converting

the guest house. Michelle says we're officially becoming that industry power couple she always knew we would be."

He pulls me close, both of us a mess of sweat and dust from moving boxes all morning. "Have I mentioned lately that you're perfect?"

"Once or twice." I lean into him, breathing in the familiar scent of him mixed with salt air. "Though I think Billboard's advance review of your new album mentioned it more."

"*Their best work yet,*" he quotes. "*A triumph of evolution while maintaining their signature sound.*' Will says they're calling it the comeback album of the decade."

"'Love songs that actually sound happy,'" I quote Will's review.

His laugh vibrates through me. "He's just mad we're making him play slower tempos."

"Poor Will."

"Poor Will who cried when we played him the final mix and then threatened to quit if we ever told anyone."

The sound of waves fills our comfortable silence. Our house. Our future. Our everything, finally aligned.

"Hey," he says suddenly. "Come watch the sunset from the deck. First one in our new home."

"Chase, we're filthy. We should shower—"

"Please?" Something in his voice makes me look

up. That subtle tell I've known for twenty years. He's up to something. For all I know there could be a new puppy out there wrapped in a cute bow.

"Okay..."

He takes my hand, leads me through empty rooms we'll soon fill with our combined lives. The deck stretches toward the ocean like reaching for infinity.

"You know what I was thinking about earlier?" he asks, pulling me close as the sun starts its descent.

"How we need furniture?"

"How twenty years ago, I walked into the Viper Room on a Tuesday night and saw this woman in killer heels watching our set. You were supposed to be somewhere else – or had an early meeting the next day, you told me later. But something made you stay."

I smile against his chest. "Something in the air. Something in the sound."

"You said we were either going to be the biggest band in the world or the biggest disaster you'd ever seen." His heart beats steady under my ear. "And now here we are. The new album's about to drop. We're in *our* house. Everything's finally... finally right."

"Finally," I agree.

He shifts, and I feel him reach into his pocket. My heart stops.

"Eliza." His voice is soft. "Look at me?"

I do. He's holding a small velvet box.

"Chase..."

"Twenty years ago, you walked into that club and

my whole life changed. You believed in our music. In me. In us. Even when I couldn't believe in myself." He opens the box. The ring catches sunset light - vintage-inspired but modern, exactly my style. "You saved my life by believing in our sound. You *literally* saved my life in Chicago. You saved it again by forcing me to face hard truths about myself when I needed to heal. And now, I think I'm done being saved. Now I want to spend the rest of my life showing you I'm worth it. All of this has been worth the wait."

Tears blur my vision as he drops to one knee.

"Marry me?" he asks simply. "Finally?"

"Yes." The word comes instantly. I don't need to think twice. Not anymore. "Yes, finally, yes."

The ring slides perfectly onto my finger. When he kisses me, it tastes like salt air and promises and twenty years of almosts turning into absolutely.

I never thought we could get here. After all this time. All the pain and heartache along the way. The trials and tribulations that kept us in each other's orbits whether we wanted it or not, and then blew us apart. And finally, a recognition ceremony that forced us to confront our entire history, bringing everything back to the surface so we could clear the way for our future.

Bringing us to now.

"I love you," he murmurs against my lips.

"I love you too."

The sun sets on our first day in our new home. Tomorrow brings movers and furniture and advance copies of the album. Next month brings the release, the tour, the future we've finally earned.

But right now...

Right now it's just us. Finally us. Completely us.

Some love stories take the scenic route. Some timing needs twenty years to get right. Some truths don't need to be whispered anymore.

They just need to be lived.

--THE END—

Living Chase Playlist

https://open.spotify.com/playlist/0UrwzEEnE
FIUcOrW3EMNsr?si=jZPzzAaIRkqRkZ3o
GzmB8w

1. *Imposter Syndrome,* Sophie Lloyd, Lzzy Hale
2. *Play the Game Tonight,* Ronnie Romero
3. *Shouldn't Be with Me,* Kami Kehoe
4. *Sin on Skin,* Those Damn Crows
5. *Hell You Call A Dream,* The Warning
6. *Bad Guy,* Falling In Reverse, Saraya
7. *Anybody,* Dead Sara
8. *Pieces,* Daughtry
9. *Run,* Plush
10. *Chains (The Tower),* Fame on Fire, SiM
11. *Don't Tell Me,* Disturbed, Ann Wilson
12. *Speechless,* 10 Years

13. *Better Days,* Staind, Dorothy
14. *The Dam,* Daughtry
15. *I Am the Fire,* Halestorm
16. *Don't Let It End,* Jeff Scott Soto, Dino Jelusick
17. *New Way Out,* Poppy
18. *The Road to Hell,* Sunstorm
19. *Can U See Me in the Dark?,* Halestorm, I Prevail
20. *Better Days,* Paralandra
21. *Alive Again,* Hartmann
22. *More,* The Warning
23. *Black Butterfly,* Scott Stapp
24. *Don't Stop the Devil,* Dead Posey
25. *Sacred Place,* Black Swan
26. *Can't Quench the Fire,* Paralandra
27. *'Cause I know You're the One,* Restless Spirits, Dino Jelusick
28. *Heaven's Got A Back Door,* Dead Sara
29. *Heart Beat Here,* Dashboard Confessional
30. *Whispered Truths,* Incendiary Ink (no recording)
31. *The Night Cries Out (For You),* Rough Cutt
32. *Never Tear Us Apart,* Bishop Briggs
33. *What Are You Waiting For,* W.E.T.
34. *Look At Me Now,* Paralandra
35. *The Best,* AWOLNATION
36. *Wildfire,* Against the Current

Thank you

If you enjoyed this book, please consider taking a moment to leave a Review. Even a star Rating helps indie authors Reach a wider audience.

goodreads   **amazon**kindle   **BookBub**

Also by Amy Booker

Near Miss RockStar Series

Almost

So Close

Barely

Near Miss Rock Star Collection

In Reach

Drive Me Wild Vegas Series

Ms. Fortune

Ms. Chief

Ms. Lead

Ms. Take

The Mischief Motors Collection

Rhapsody RockStar Series

Coda

Reprise

Overture

Waltz

Sustain

Chaos Fuel RockStar Series

Mayhem

Madness

Incendiary Ink Rockstar Series

Giving Chase

Contact Amy

FOLLOW

My website: http://www.amybookerauthor.com
Facebook: www.facebook.com/amybookerauthor
Instagram: www.instagram.com/amy_booker_author/
TikTok: www.TikTok.com/@amybookerauthor
Goodreads: www.goodreads.com/author/show/
22225202.Amy_Booker
Amazon: https://rebrand.ly/sraegoj

BUY DIRECT

Amy Booker Store: https://payhip.com/AmyBooker

INTERACT

Email: amybookerauthor@gmail.com
Facebook Reader Group: https://www.facebook.com/groups/amybookersroadies
Newsletter Sign Up: https://www.amybookerauthor.com/subscribe

READ EARLY

Join my ARC Team: https://forms.gle/Ns1QKmrrsQz4ay5S6